"A massage before your speech might relax you, Erica."

Oh, sure, Erica thought. She knew her self-control would vanish if she allowed him to touch her. But his idea *did* sound enticing. "Okay, Nick, you're on." She walked into her bedroom and stretched out facedown on the bed. "I'm ready."

Nick sat beside her and ran a fingertip along her spine. "So am I." He placed his hands lightly on either side of her waist, his thumbs toward her spine, and kneaded his way up her back. "Relax, Erica."

She groaned inwardly. His hands felt *so* wonderful. "I'm trying."

"Your upper back feels like steel." He held her shoulders and lowered his head to within a few inches of her face. "Take deep breaths," he instructed. And she strove for inner calm....

After a few moments Erica wondered why Nick had stopped massaging her. "More, please," she gasped, and just as she turned her head to look up at him, his lips met hers....

Cassie Miles found researching and writing *Monkey Business*, her fifth Temptation, both thought-provoking and amusing. She says she became aware of "the educational significance of primate studies and also of the devastating fact that chimps and gorillas are endangered species." One of the organizations dedicated to studying and preserving nonhuman primates, which Cassie would like to acknowledge, is The Jane Goodall Institute, P.O. Box 26846, Tucson, AZ 85726-6846.

Cassie lives in Denver, Colorado, with her husband and their two daughters.

Books by Cassie Miles

HARLEQUIN TEMPTATION

26–TONGUE-TIED
61–ACTS OF MAGIC
104–IT'S ONLY NATURAL
170–SEEMS LIKE OLD TIMES

Monkey Business

CASSIE MILES

Harlequin Books

TORONTO • NEW YORK • LONDON
AMSTERDAM • PARIS • SYDNEY • HAMBURG
STOCKHOLM • ATHENS • TOKYO • MILAN

Published January 1989

ISBN 0-373-25335-4

1

THE HAIRY BEAST PEERED from beneath the primrose dust ruffle on Erica Swanson's bed. A prism of late-afternoon sunlight slanted through the window onto the hardwood floor, and the creature reached toward the sharp edge of light.

There was a sound. Quickly the long knobby fingers withdrew, and the beast was utterly still.

Erica paused in the bedroom doorway, too preoccupied with the envelope in her hand to be aware of anything else. The return address read International Exploration and Excursion. This was a letter she'd been waiting for. She took a deep breath, crossed her fingers and shivered as an eerie intuition came over her, a prickly sensation, as if someone or something were watching her. Her brown-eyed gaze flicked around the room. Nonsense! She shrugged off the feeling and ripped open the envelope.

"Damn." Another rejection to her grant proposal. She crumpled the paper and threw it on the floor.

Silently the beast watched.

With a sigh Erica plodded across the room to her four-poster bed, sat on the edge and untied her Adidas. She'd struck out with International Exploration, but it wasn't her last chance. Two other grant-proposal inquiries hadn't yet been answered. She wearily let her shoe plop on the floor.

A sinewed, hairy arm crept from under the bed and snagged the first sneaker. It vanished beneath the yellow dust ruffle.

Erica dropped her other shoe.

The arm appeared again. Long, prehensile fingers moved slowly, stealthily, until Erica's leg was within their grasp. A sudden jerk. The fingers encircled her ankle.

With a shriek Erica leaped to her feet. Off balance, she fell back, clutching at the pale yellow coverlet. Her leg was captured in a tight inhuman grasp. She lay back on the bed and screamed . . . with laughter.

"Sheena, you silly chimp. You scared me."

The three-year-old chimpanzee responded with a hee-hee-hoot, released her keeper's ankle and emerged from under the bed. Her loose lips flapped, and she made a noise much like a chuckle.

"Very cute." Erica's voice was heavy with sarcasm.

Sheena's head drooped, but Erica didn't mistake this pose for repentance. During the three months she'd been taking Sheena home from Golden Independent Zoo west of Denver, she'd learned that apology was not among the chimp's repertoire of responses.

Panting and hooting, Sheena hopped onto the bed beside Erica and began picking through and grooming her keeper's short chestnut-brown curls.

"You're not supposed to be in here," Erica chided fondly. "My bedroom is strictly off-limits to chimps."

Had Sheena done any damage? Erica scanned the bedroom. Everything seemed to be in order. The spindle-sided bookshelf was still standing. The vase of daisies on the dresser hadn't been eaten. Most important, Sheena hadn't dismantled Erica's glittering display of glass animals, a collection that included one piece for each year of her life. An owl symbolized the year she'd graduated from college. A dove was for the year she'd married. A jackal for the divorce. Altogether there were thirty-two animals. Three were chimps.

When Sheena knuckled across the room to snatch the wadded-up letter, her keeper gave a resigned sigh. "You may have that."

Promptly Sheena popped the paper into her mouth.

"You may play with it, but please don't eat it."

Sheena chomped the letter between her strong teeth and grinned, showing Erica the crumpled wad.

"Don't eat it, Sheena. Rejections are probably poisonous." Erica made a grab that the ape easily evaded. Though Sheena was only twenty-eight inches tall and weighed only thirty-five pounds, she could easily outmaneuver a Harlem Globetrotter.

"Come on, let's get out of the bedroom." Erica made chimpish grunts, sounds that meant "good food," as she strode to the door. "Ready for dinner? Some nice, yummy Monkey Mash?"

When Sheena followed in her knuckle-dragging, bow-legged gait, Erica doubled back to close and lock the bedroom door.

That was easy, too easy. Sheena wasn't usually distracted by such a simple ploy. Erica presumed that the chimp was plotting other devilment, like flooding the bathtub or eating the drapes. Halfway down the hall, Erica turned up the air-conditioning, which seemed to have two speeds—either too high or too low. Still, Erica couldn't complain because this apartment building was owned by Amanda Hatfield, the woman who also owned the zoo where Erica had worked for the past year and a half. It was unlikely that any other landlady would have been willing to permit a tenant to have an animal such as Sheena stay there without collecting a sufficient damage deposit.

While Sheena turned somersaults on the grass mats spread across the living-room floor, Erica sat in a chimp-battered chair and peeled off the navy knee socks that matched the shirt and shorts of her zoo uniform. Bare-foot, she padded to the kitchen area of her two-bedroom apartment.

In the refrigerator were apples, peaches, oranges and lettuce. A marvelous array if you happened to be a hun-gry jungle primate. "Looks like fruit salad," she said. "Again."

As Erica selected peaches and apples, she watched Sheena, who had abandoned the scrap of paper in favor of bashing her stuffed monkey doll. Not love taps, but a wild, rambunctious flinging. Then she calmed, embraced the doll and kissed it in a parody of true love.

"You're too young for mating urges."

Ignoring her keeper's comments, Sheena slobbered kisses on her doll.

"Really, Sheena. You won't be adolescent for another four years. You're much too young to have a lover. A chimp companion, however, would be wonderful."

Since mid-April Erica had been trying to integrate Sheena into the four-member tribe of chimps at the zoo. Though Primate Island wasn't exactly a return to the wild, the environment was as near to a natural habitat as pos-sible for a chimpanzee in Colorado. On the island Sheena would be with her own kind; possibly she would mate and find satisfying bonds with the other chimps. Unfortu-nately Erica's plans were failing miserably. Every day she escorted Sheena across the moat to the island. Every day the little chimp ended her close encounter of the ape kind with hysterical shrieks.

Erica sighed when Sheena looked up at her and made the hoot for food. "I wish you communicated as well with the other chimps as you do with me."

Because her goal was to have Sheena return to her own kind, Erica avoided the use of sign language. At first she'd tried not to verbalize except for chimpish sounds, but Sheena seemed to be so distressed with that behavior that Erica relented to normal human conversation. "Oh, Sheena. Wouldn't you rather have a chimp friend? There's a male on the island who's just your age. Remember? His name's Java."

The wishful cajoling sounded pathetic, even to Erica. She knew as well as anyone that relationships couldn't be forced. Still, she couldn't help encouraging the chimp. "It'd be great fun."

Sheena shook her head vigorously.

"You don't believe that?"

Sheena hooted.

"Believe it, Sheena. Someday you'll meet a Prince Charming—maybe even Java—and you'll live happily ever after."

Sheena's hooting accelerated.

"Don't believe that, either, huh?" Matter-of-factly Erica added, "Nor do I. I guess neither of us is the Cinderella type. Which is just as well. I don't imagine that glass slippers come in your size."

The chimp bounded onto the kitchen counter and grasped a peach. Tightly. The delicate fruit oozed between her fingers.

Erica chose not to scold. Squishing a peach was no big deal, and a more emphatic response might encourage further antics. When the chimp snatched a ceramic jar from the countertop, however, Erica snapped a reprimand. "Put that down."

Sheena did. With a crash. The jar broke, scattering oatmeal across the tile floor. She lifted another container. Erica grabbed at the same time, underlining her action with a threatening hoot. They struggled for a moment. Sheena won, and the container of Monkey Mash hurled to the floor.

"Stop it! You know better than this."

Sheena chattered her teeth.

"Don't you dare talk back to me!" Then Erica groaned. "What am I saying? You're not talking back. You're an ape. You can't talk. I'm the one who's going bananas."

Sheena sprang to the windowsill and balanced with her long toes gripping the ledge. Erica didn't like the way the chimp was studying the flip lock on the window. "Come on, Sheena. Move away from there."

Sheena screwed her face into an expression that obviously meant Drop dead, Erica. She deftly unhitched the lock and slid the window open.

Erica froze. "Very clever, Sheena. I didn't know you'd figured out that lock. But—thank God!—there's still a screen in the way." She offered a friendly smile and held out her arms. "If you come here, I promise to take you for a ride. In your car seat? Would you like that?"

Apparently Sheena wasn't interested because she flipped the catch on the screen and leaped through the second-story window.

Erica dove for the window. "Sheena!"

Only a few feet away—but out of reach—Sheena dangled from the thick branches of a tall cottonwood tree. Without so much as a wave goodbye she agilely descended.

Erica raced to the door. Shoes, she remembered. She fled down the short hallway to her bedroom, struggled with the lock and dashed inside. There was the left shoe. She jammed her foot into it. Where was her other shoe? On hands and knees she slid under the bed, feeling, grasping, searching for her sneaker. It was wedged between the night table and the bed. She wriggled out from under the bed, cursing. Sheena could be in Kansas by now.

Erica grabbed the chimp's shoulder harness and leash and flew from her apartment, down the stairs and out the front entrance, where she was struck by the dry heat of a July afternoon. Rounding the brick apartment building, she stared. There was the cottonwood. There was the open window to her apartment. But no Sheena.

She ran to the parking lot. An elderly gentleman was climbing out of his sedan, and Erica accosted him. "Have you seen a chimpanzee?"

"I sure have. Back in the summer of '83. At the zoo."

Erica sprinted from the parking lot to the street. Cars. There were so many cars. In one direction was a quiet residential area. The other led to a busy street. Would Sheena have the sense to avoid traffic? No way, Erica decided. She aimed for the hectic boulevard.

At the corner she met two kids with bikes. "A chimp?" Erica gasped. "Did you see a chimp?"

"Nope," said one, "but I sure saw a monkey."

"It looked like it was going to Barron's."

He pointed down the sidewalk. Sheena was nowhere in sight, but two blocks away Erica saw the pastel neon sign for Barron's Gardens and Amusement Park.

Erica took off at a run. Shoving through the few pedestrians, she passed the first stoplight. The second. Across the busy street. To Barron's. Mingled with the noise of street traffic, she heard the rumble of a roller coaster, squeals of delight and a tinkling musical sound. An organ-grinder?

Outside the entry to Barron's an elaborately musta-chioed man with massive black curls stood in the midst of several giggling children. Raising his hand from the organ-grinder box, he waved to Erica. "Hey, lady. You lose a monkey?"

"Yes." Breathing heavily, she strode toward him, peering over the heads of the laughing children. In the center of their circle Sheena bounced on her knuckles and made silly faces.

Erica glared.

Sheena glared back. With a screech the chimp hurled herself into the organ-grinder's arms.

"Please hold on to her," Erica shouted.

Her warning was unnecessary. Sheena had a stranglehold on the man's neck. As Erica approached with the shoulder harness, Sheena scrambled onto his shoulders. Her hoots and shrieks were a perfect imitation of terror. Erica was furious. For three months she'd disrupted her life, made a home for Sheena and cared for her. Now the ungrateful creature was acting like a battered chimp.

One of the children informed her, "The monkey doesn't want to go with you."

"Yeah," chimed in another. "It's scared of you."

The organ-grinder had a solution. "Give me the leash. I'll put it on her."

Though Erica would have preferred to handle the situation herself, Sheena had stretched to her full height on the man's shoulders and was staring at the silver-leaved branches of a Russian olive tree. Another escape route? Erica tossed the harness and leash to the organ-grinder. After contending with a tangle of arms and legs, the man was able to fit the harness across Sheena's chest and buckle it behind her back.

The children cheered.

"Thank you," Erica said as she wrapped the end of the leash firmly around her wrist. "Let's go, Sheena."

Sheena had no intention of going quietly. Erica gave a tug. Sheena tugged back. Now the chimp was even more agitated. Much to the delight of the children, she hooked her legs around the organ-grinder's neck and made wild, flinging gestures with her long arms.

Erica gave a loud, threatening hoot.

Immediately the children imitated her.

Sheena pursed her lips and wailed.

"A suggestion?" the organ-grinder said. "Let's find a more quiet place, and maybe she'll calm down."

Erica threw up her arms in frustration. "All right."

As soon as she handed the leash back to the organ-grinder and took his music box, Sheena seemed to relax. She snuggled in the man's arms and gave him a rubber-lipped kiss.

A mating urge? Erica wondered with acute annoyance.

Apart from that incredible hair and the mustache—both of which were no doubt, Erica thought fake—this man didn't resemble an ape. Though it was difficult to assess his body under the baggy organ-grinder's costume, he didn't appear to have arms down to his knees or widely bowed legs. He wasn't walking on his knuckles. Dark hair glistened on his tanned forearms, but there certainly wasn't enough fur to qualify for apehood. Erica gritted her teeth. It was just like Sheena to fall for someone totally out of her species.

The organ-grinder waved farewell to the children at the gate, a gesture that Sheena copied. Then he escorted Erica toward the entry gate for Barron's Gardens.

She balked. "I thought you said a quiet place."

"I did."

"Much as I hate to belabor the obvious, this is an amusement park, with crowds, rides and very little quiet."

"You're right about that."

She studied his expression. Usually she was an excellent judge of character—human and/or primate—but this man baffled her. Was he leading her on a wild chimp chase? And what on earth did he look like under that droopy mustache?

"It's not the public library," he continued, "but I do know a corner of Barron's that isn't noisy. Trust me."

Why not? Sheena did. Yet that ought to be a clue. Most of the time Sheena's judgment was worth considerably less than a bowl of Monkey Mash. Still, Erica fell into step beside the organ-grinder. What choice was there? She couldn't very well drag Sheena, screaming and kicking, through the streets of Denver. They could both be seriously injured in such an attempt.

Once inside the gates Erica discovered that Barron's Gardens and Amusement Park wasn't what she'd expected. She'd assumed there would be a chaotic midway, cotton candy and garish rides. Instead the entry led past two beautifully landscaped miniature golf courses. Apparently Barron's took the "garden" part of its title seriously.

"I have the advantage," the organ-grinder said.

"You also have the chimp."

"I meant that I know your name is Erica and you work at Golden Independent Zoo."

Erica glanced down at the name stitched above her left breast pocket. The patch for the zoo was on her sleeve. "I know you work here. And judging by your ability to soothe this savage beast, your name might be Tarzan."

"But it isn't. I'm Nick Barron."

"Related to the Barron who owns this place?"

"I *am* the Barron. The third generation of Barron actually."

"Congratulations. Your park seems very nice and well kept. Though I don't generally frequent this sort of place."

"Why not?"

"Oh, please." Erica drew a breath and tried not to be rude. The man had leashed Sheena, after all. "I'm a little too old for rides on a roller coaster."

Nick indicated a white-haired couple who were playing miniature golf. "You're only as old as you feel."

"Today I feel like Methuselah. Not only has it been incredibly hot, but one of the llamas spit on me when I was cleaning their pen, I fell in the moat around Primate Island and my favorite buffalo is sick. Not to mention Sheena's escape. And the rejection letter from International Exploration."

She clamped her mouth shut. It wasn't like her to confide in a complete stranger.

"Go ahead," he urged. "Continue."

It wasn't doing a thing for her already dismal mood that everyone they passed stopped and stared. "I've said enough. Why don't you tell me about your park?"

"Barron's was founded fifty-two years ago as a botanical sanctuary. When my grandfather opened the Gardens, there was only a little restaurant and a bandstand. Years later he added a carousel."

They left the shaded miniature golf course and stepped onto the bright, crowded midway, where colorful rides swirled and costumed vendors plied customers with hot dogs and pretzels. Roaring mechanical laughter came from a Fun House whose entrance was a man-size mouth. The patrons squealed as they were swooped sky-high or swizzled in circles. Even Sheena was astounded. Erica beheld the spectacle with a wry grin. "A sanctuary?"

"Not anymore. Not unless you consider the all-American fun seeker as an endangered species. My father was the P. T. Barnum who added the Fun House, Ferris wheel and roller coaster." He directed her through a colorful portal marked Kiddy Land, where the thrills and chills were scaled down to child-size. "This way."

"And what about you? Barnum or botanist?"

"A little of both. My policy is to keep Barron's quiet enough for family picnics but large enough to run at a profit."

Sheena made her pant-hooting noise.

"Oh, yes," Erica said. "The hairy little monster who seems to have taken a fancy to you is named Sheena."

"A pet?"

"Certainly not." Erica was instantly offended. She didn't approve of wild animals as pets. Today's escapade proved the idiocy of such endeavors. "I'm trying to convince Sheena that she wants to join the other chimps on Primate Island at the zoo."

"You have several chimps? Do you ever rent them out?"

She was appalled at the suggestion. "No. They're not a performing troupe. At the zoo we're trying to create as natural an environment as possible."

"Too bad. Old Sheena liked playing with the kids. She's really responsive."

"Chimps are like that. They're very social, but—"

"Then why not let them enjoy themselves?"

"Because it's not the natural order of things." This was a familiar and complex argument, one that she'd considered from several angles before accepting the position at the zoo. She did not, however, intend to seriously explain her philosophies to a man who hid behind a droopy fake mustache.

"Natural order," he mused. "Are you telling me it's not natural to enjoy yourself?"

"Of course not. And I don't appreciate the way you're twisting my words."

"Why shouldn't Sheena play with kids if it makes her happy?"

"For one thing, humans aren't truly capable of knowing the emotional state of a chimpanzee. How can we tell if she's happy? Or frightened? Another reason Sheena shouldn't play with children is that she's strong enough to break their little arms if she doesn't like the game."

That slowed him down but didn't stop him. "What about performing?" he asked. "Sheena seems to like attention."

"Listen, Nick, I have a B.A. in biology and a Master's in anthropology with emphasis on primatology. I've been to Fossey's gorilla camp in Rwanda and Goodall's camp on the Gombe River. I am currently engaged in research on parenting-bonding instincts among apes in captivity. I know what's best for Sheena."

He directed her along a narrow, cobblestoned pathway surrounded by lilac bushes. "I can't help but notice," he remarked, "that Sheena doesn't seem to be staying where she belongs—according to your idea of natural order."

Touché, Mr. Organ-Grinder. "Sheena was brought up by human beings. She has difficulty interpreting chimp behavior."

"She doesn't like it," he summarized. "But I guess an expert like you knows what's best."

He opened the rear door to a narrow, two-story replica of a Dutch windmill. It was brightly painted and surrounded by tulips all in a row. But there was nothing cutesy about the interior. The carpet was a rich mocha, several shades darker than the paneling on the walls. A circular brass staircase swirled beside the door. The furnishings—cabinets, files, leather chairs and a desk—exuded masculinity. "My office," he said, closing the door behind her, since the place was air-conditioned.

The cool silence that enveloped them was incredible. Erica could hear herself breathe. Nick Barron was an irritating man, but his office showed definite redeeming qualities. "You were right about one thing," she admitted. "It's quiet in here."

"We're talking industrial strength soundproofing. When you grow up under a roller coaster, you learn to appreciate stillness."

Sheena hopped out of his arms. When Erica undid her leash, she began circling the room.

"Make yourself at home," he said, stepping behind the desk. He whipped off the frizzy organ grinder's wig to reveal his own sandy-brown hair, which was neatly trimmed and not so curly.

Erica relaxed in one of the comfortable leather chairs as she watched him. Finally it was time for that idiot mustache to be removed. The prospect of seeing his face pleased her, but she couldn't say why.

He massaged his scalp with his hand. "Feels good to get that thing off. Wigs are hot in July."

"I'll bet the mustache is hot, too."

He wiggled his nose. "Nope, the mustache is just silly."

"Aren't you going to take it off?"

He raised his eyebrows as he regarded her. She had the disconcerting sense that he was noticing her for the first time. And that he was not displeased. "Do you want me to take it off?"

She avoided his mocking gaze and his tone, which suggested stripping off a far more intimate article.

"Come on, Erica, shall I take it off?"

"I don't care." But she did. She was dying to see his real upper lip, but wouldn't give him the satisfaction of admitting it. "Doesn't matter to me whether you take it off or leave it on or have it bronzed."

"Not even a little bit curious?"

"Not really."

She affected an attitude of unconcern when she noticed the mischievous glow in his light brown eyes. No wonder he and Sheena got along so well.

His gaze slid over her body. "I do admire your credentials, Erica. But I thought anthropologists were supposed to be curious."

Sheena skittered up to the desk and grabbed the curly wig.

"Sheena," Erica scolded. "Give that back."

"It's okay. She can play with it."

Erica started to object, then stopped herself. It'd serve him right if Sheena demolished his ridiculous wig. Besides, he wouldn't believe her if she warned him. He seemed to take exception to every word she uttered. She'd met Nick only a few minutes ago, and they'd already disagreed about practically everything. They seemed to rub each other the wrong way, like two pieces of flint striking sparks.

"Would you care for a soda pop?" he asked.

She didn't like carbonated beverages, didn't consider the ingredients healthy. "I'd prefer water. With ice."

"Really? I drink a six-pack a day of pop."

That figured. He'd say "to-may-to." She'd say "to-mah-to."

After a teasing twitch of his mustache he opened a half-size, paneled refrigerator that was tucked neatly beneath a small wet bar. Instantly Sheena was beside him. With lightning speed the chimp reached inside and seized an apple. Nick made a grab for her and missed by a mile. Finally, Erica thought, they had something in common: he was as helpless at catching Sheena as she was.

"Is she allowed to eat apples?"

"Yes. Her diet is quite similar to ours."

Sheena swung onto the circular staircase and settled down to nibble her apple with ladylike bites, alternating between that and plucking at the curly dark wig. This was the most calm she'd been all day.

Erica, on the other hand, was experiencing a perverse agitation. Nick's presence provoked an uncomfortable prickling along her arms and a tension in her stomach. Of course, these wriggly sensations weren't unfamiliar to her. She knew her body well enough to recognize the symptoms of animal attraction. The well-known mating urge, she thought as she accepted a glass of ice water from him. "Thank you."

He braced his arm across the back of her chair, leaned down and clinked glasses with her. He was near enough that she could smell his spicy after-shave.

"Here's to the very natural function of having fun," he said.

Erica forced herself not to return what she supposed was a smile under that grotesque mustache. He was awfully sure of himself, and the way her body was responding confirmed his right to be confident. What a bother! She didn't want to have the hots for Nick, the amusement park Barron. Her future plans didn't include a man. A mate? She almost choked on her ice water. What was she thinking about?

She ordered herself to relax, to grow up, to behave like a mature female. But her eyes betrayed her. She couldn't stop staring at him as he tilted his head back and drank the fizzing liquid in his glass.

He knew she was watching, and that irritated her even more. Wasn't that always the way with the dominant male in a tribe? Being infuriatingly sure of himself? She remembered her observations of chimps in the wild. Whenever a female was in heat, the dominant male waded through his lesser companions and asserted his masculine rights. Even without further study Erica was certain that Nick would be the leader of whichever pack he joined. That was fine for him, but she most certainly didn't intend to be a complacent conquest.

She glanced up at him, smiling sweetly. With a flick of her wrist she peeled the mustache off his upper lip.

"Ow!" He jerked away in surprise.

"Isn't that better?" she teased. "More natural?"

Oh, wow, she thought, he had a great mouth. Full, well-shaped lips that perfectly complemented his strong features.

"I'm amazed," he said with a glower. "I didn't think proper anthropologist ladies did things like that."

"Sometimes the usually submissive female primate finds aggression to be a necessary behavior."

"A warning?"

She knew he'd gotten the message. Erica Swanson, intelligent twentieth-century female, was not about to be overcome by her mating urge. Not when she and the male in question so clearly had nothing in common.

He rubbed the place where his mustache had been. "How much biology do you know, Erica?"

"Why do you ask?"

"All my life I've been allergic to furbearing animals. And our little buddy over there was climbing all over me. But I don't have a rash. And my eyes aren't watering, are they?"

She peered into his light brown eyes. They weren't teary. They were flecked with gold. "Your eyes are fine."

"Why is that?"

"Possibly Sheena's fur is a type that doesn't affect you. I really don't know much about this, but sometimes people outgrow allergies. Body chemistry changes."

"I hope that's it. I've always wanted to get a dog. Maybe now is the time."

"You never had pets?"

"Never did."

She couldn't imagine it. Back home in rural Wisconsin, her large family had always kept a series of dogs, cats, parakeets, gerbils and bunnies, as well as the livestock. Erica, who was smack in the middle of the seven Swanson children, sometimes thought of the animals as her *real* family. The cocker spaniel always had time to play with her. And the blue budgie always chirped an answer when Erica confided in him. Growing up without them would have been terribly lonely, in spite of the constant human activity within the Swanson home.

She softened toward Nick. Perhaps the lack of pets while growing up made him contentious, overly anxious to dominate.

"Maybe I'll have to get a chimp," he said.

Erica's newborn sympathies hardened to granite. "Don't be ridiculous. Chimps aren't pets, unless you live in a jungle. That's what happened to Sheena."

From the chimp on the staircase there came a pant-hoot in response to her name.

Erica continued. "A very nice man brought Sheena home with him from Africa when she was six months old. Apparently he took very good care of her, but Sheena got bigger and began acting like an animal. He finally tired of never being able to entertain and of having to replace his furniture every other month. The result—he feels awful about giving Sheena up, and Sheena is unable to integrate into a tribe of her own species."

"All right. You've convinced me. Chimps aren't pets."

"Surprising sensitivity for someone who thinks it's amusing to dress up as an organ-grinder." Erica paused. Since when was she so pompous and self-righteous? Her usual manner was tolerant, but there was something about Nick that seemed to demand extreme behavior. She fought it; her tone was almost conciliatory as she said, "You probably didn't know, but organ-grinders were notorious for mistreating their monkeys."

Nick spread his arms wide in a mocking, expansive apology. "You're right. I didn't know."

Sheena darted from the staircase and patted his arm.

"Sheena forgives me," he said.

"Sheena has no idea what we're talking about." Erica rose to her feet. The best thing to do was extricate herself from this situation before it got any stickier. "But she does seem to have calmed down. Thank you, Nick, for your help with her. Now, I think it's time for us to go home."

She held out her hand to the chimp.

Sheena looked at Erica, then at Nick. Very carefully she took Nick's hand and placed it in Erica's. After a few grunts while she held their hands together she scampered back to the staircase to play with the wig.

His flesh was warm, his grasp firm. Erica looked from their clasped hands to his gold-flecked eyes. Her intellect told her to take her hand away, but she was riveted palm to palm by an irresistible charge. Nick squeezed lightly. Without thinking Erica squeezed back.

"Maybe," he drawled, "Sheena knows more than you or I."

"Instinct," Erica said, then quickly wished she hadn't. Her crazed mating urges were giving her enough trouble. Though she released his hand, the sense of being connected remained. "I really have to be going."

"Let me drive you."

She nodded, then wondered, where was her brain? Her sense of self-preservation? Getting involved with this man was possibly the dumbest thing she could ever do.

As they led a docile Sheena through the park to Nick's van, confusion predominated in her mind. How could she be attracted to such an inappropriate mate? Only marginally aware of her surroundings, Erica issued the directions to her apartment.

It wasn't until she opened the unlocked door of her apartment that she returned to reality with a thud. Ah, yes, here was the beat-up furniture, Sheena's clutter, the wadded-up rejection letter. This was not the home of a woman who dined by candlelight and lost glass slippers. If she wanted to see Nick again, she should simply blurt it out. But did she dare?

He grinned at her. "Charming place you've got here."

"The decor is primate primitive."

Sheena flopped on the floor, staring up at the ceiling. Her posture suggested complete exhaustion. And Erica agreed. It had been a long, hot, disconcerting day.

Erica marched into the kitchen and firmly closed the window. Nick followed. She could tell he was trying not to laugh as he beheld the broken jars. "Could I offer you ladies dinner at my place? Of course, I should warn you that my son, Michael, is cooking tonight. Our kitchen could look worse than this."

"Your son?" He wasn't married, was he?

"Michael. He's sixteen."

That wasn't what she wanted to know. "Are you . . . ?"

"His mother and I have been divorced for seven years." His lips curved in a rueful smile. "What about you, Erica? Is there someone in your life besides Sheena?"

"Two parents. Six siblings. But Sheena and I live alone."

"Then how about dinner?"

"I would like that very much." What was she saying? Quickly she added, "But not tonight, Nick."

"Another time?"

"Yes." She was pleased there would be another time. This first encounter had gotten off to the worst—and the best—start imaginable.

She walked him to the door. "Still no allergy rashes?"

"Nothing yet," he informed her. "That's a good sign. Maybe I'm entering a new phase of my life."

The door closed behind him and Erica leaned against it. Much to her surprise, she was hoping that Nick's new phase of life would include her.

2

THAT NIGHT WAS NOT a fantasy-filled, sleepless tossing and turning. After cleaning up the mess in the kitchen, hammering makeshift locks to the windows, feeding Sheena and tucking the little chimp into her hammock, Erica was too exhausted for dreams. She dragged off her zoo uniform and fell into bed, forgoing her nightly ritual of listening to pleasantly mind-numbing rock music through her Walkman headphones.

It wasn't until the next morning at Golden Independent Zoo that Erica took a hard look at her attraction to Nick. She knew it was wisest to look before she leaped. A blind leap could lead to a painful fall, and she wasn't at all sure what she was leaping into. A relationship? Impossible!

Her career left neither time nor energy for a commitment. Not only was she busy at the zoo, but as soon as one of her grant proposals was accepted, she intended to be off to Africa for an extended period of primatological field study. Starting a relationship wouldn't be fair. It wouldn't be right.

After pulling high rubber boots on over her sneakers, she pushed a wheelbarrow of feed up the hill toward the llama enclosure. True, she'd been fascinated by Nick. But that didn't necessarily mean they had to have a *real* relationship. How could they, when they had so very little in common? All they seemed to share was lust. A pure and simple sexual attraction—if there was anything pure and simple about that.

Should she leap into a wild, wanton fling? Erica frowned as she dumped feed into the llamas' trough and turned on the hose. She wasn't the type of person who enjoyed a casual affair. One of her worst faults, in fact, was taking things too seriously.

On the other hand, lust was natural, a scientifically measurable phenomenon. Since her divorce three years ago, she'd had only one brief involvement with another man. Hormonal urges were to be expected. Biology could not be denied forever.

She finished mucking out the reindeer enclosure, then started back down the hill, pausing beside the waist-high concrete wall surrounding the groundhog community. The fat, furry rodents bustled over and around the mounds of dirt, through their interconnecting network of tunnels. Despite their zippy activity, their lives were blissfully uncomplicated—eat, sleep, mate and eat some more. Only humans made natural instincts so complex.

At the door to the main office she considered that maybe this worry was needless. Maybe he wouldn't even call her. She shook her head. He'd call. From years of observing higher primate behavior, she could assume that any healthy male, like Nick, was ever ready to assert his masculinity in a primitive, physical manner. Higher primates? Primitive physicality? Good grief, when had she become such a prude? *Sex* was the accurate word. Men were always ready for sex and, judging from her response to him the day before, so was she.

Erica tugged off her boots, wiped her sneakers on the Welcome mat and entered the Golden Independent Zoo's main office, a rustic ranch-style cabin.

The husky voice of Amanda Hatfield, the zoo owner, intruded upon her thoughts. "Erica, my dear, what's going on?"

"Pardon me?"

"A Speedy messenger just delivered bananas for Sheena."

Erica laughed when she read the card attached to the giant banana stalk.

Thank you for an unusual afternoon.

                                        Signed,
    the man who will never be an organ-grinder again.

A banana thank-you was cute, endearing and confusing. What sort of relationship did a stalk of bananas portend?

Amanda tilted back in the swivel chair behind her desk and folded her hands beneath the braided, silver bun at her nape. "Are the bananas from your crazy sister Elaine?"

"They're from a former organ-grinder."

Erica plunked herself down behind her own desk and busily sorted through papers. Beneath her no-nonsense attitude Amanda was an incurable romantic who thought of mating urges as "true love." Erica didn't wish to encourage romantic matchmaking.

"Is this a male organ-grinder?" Amanda asked.

"Maybe."

"Please don't be coy. Have you met someone special?"

"Have I?" Erica wrinkled her forehead in mock concentration. "I'm not sure. Maybe they're from Sheena's special someone. She's been hanging out in singles' bars, you know."

"It will do you no good to be evasive, my dear."

"All right, I'll come clean. Yesterday I met a man."

"It's about time! Tell me all about him."

Erica described the events of the previous afternoon. Though she tried to dwell on her concern about Sheena's ability to escape, Amanda dragged her inexorably back to the subject of Nick Barron. What was he like? He wasn't married, was he? Did he have a sense of humor?

Erica nodded as she remembered Nick's infuriating penchant for teasing. "Yes, he has a sense of humor."

"But?" Amanda questioned as she came around her desk and stood looking out the front window. "There's a 'but' in your voice. Something you're not sure about."

"But we don't have anything in common. My life is dedicated to primatological studies. He runs an amusement park and dresses up in funny costumes."

"He sounds like exactly the sort of man you need."

"Amanda, we disagreed from the moment we met. From drinking soda pop to the importance of a natural habitat for Sheena."

"But he still got under your skin," Amanda concluded as she peered through the front window of the office. "Can't say as I blame you, Erica. I suppose he's a little taller than average height. With sandy-brown hair. And a very nice smile."

"How did you know that?"

"He's walking up the path to the office right now."

Nick? Erica turned her neck to see through the window, recognized him and sank down behind her desk. As she riffled through papers, she glanced up at Amanda's amused expression. "Don't you dare," Erica warned. "Don't play matchmaker."

"My darling girl, I obviously won't need to." Amanda swung open the door to the office, offering a friendly handshake as she and Nick introduced themselves to each other.

Erica was surprised when she saw him, surprised and fascinated. Without the baggy organ-grinder costume, he seemed taller than he had the day before. More dominant? Definitely more physically appealing. He wore a blue cotton shirt, khaki walking shorts and loafers without socks. It was an unremarkable casual outfit, but one that suited him well. His legs were well muscled and tanned. His shoulders were broad but not massive. He looked capable, she decided. A fine, mature male of the species.

"Erica?" Amanda said in cue.

"Hi, Nick," she responded quickly. Too quickly? She felt like a Peeping Thomasina who had been caught looking. "Thanks for the bananas."

"You're welcome."

His smile didn't reveal a thing, but she wondered if he could read her mind. Did he know she was lusting in her heart?

He crossed to her desk and placed a large shopping bag upon it. "The bananas are for Sheena. This is for you."

She pulled a large, stainless-steel canister from the bag. Inside was a smaller container and another and another. There were six altogether. "Very practical. I needed these," she approved. "Though you really shouldn't have, thank you."

"I didn't think you were the flowers-and-candy type."

"You're correct. Bananas and canisters are far more appreciated."

Amanda interrupted. "It occurs to me that Nick and I are in the same business—the park business. He displays flora. I display fauna. Erica, would you show Nick around? He might be able to offer some suggestions for improvements."

"I'd be really pleased to take the grand tour," he said, "but I doubt that I'll have useful advice. I don't know much about animals."

"But you do know about traffic patterns and the arrangement of a park. Don't deny it, young man. My late husband and I used to visit Barron's frequently, and I don't mind telling you that my memories are pleasant. We'd picnic on the grounds, then cuddle on a park bench, listening to the music from the bandstand. Sometimes they had harps and violins."

"Yes," Nick said, "I remember."

A gentleness edged into Amanda's husky voice, and Erica was touched by the older woman's fond memories as she described the fragrance of magnolias in spring and the carousel rides and the starlit view from the top of the Ferris wheel. Through Amanda's eyes she glimpsed a rosy, gentle past, a time she had never experienced but could imagine.

While Amanda reminisced, Erica allowed her own thoughts to wander. Her memories didn't include the unbearable sweetness of romance. Not even when she was married . . . especially not when she was married.

Her ex-husband had been a renowned, dedicated archaeologist. From a logical standpoint, he and Erica had been well matched. Though she was sometimes overpowered by his vast accomplishments, he'd been generous regarding her primatology studies. His connections had opened doors for Erica when they'd journeyed together to Africa. Yet they'd grown apart. Their career paths had taken unpredictable twists that led to long separations. Though they had many common interests, there was an absence of sharing, a core of loneliness in their relationship. Maybe if they'd taken more rides on a carousel . . .

Abruptly Amanda snapped back to the present. "Erica, show this young man around."

"Sure thing." Erica blinked away her own remembrances. "We'll be back in an hour."

She led Nick into the Colorado sunlight. A dry warmth penetrated her limbs as they strolled along the asphalt path toward the camel enclosure. Even when the temperature hit ninety, it never felt hot in these arid foothills west of Denver. Toward the north she noticed dark clouds massing for a cooling afternoon rainfall.

"I like your boss lady," he said.

Boss? Erica bristled. Despite the clever presents, he could be the most annoying man, always managing to find just the *wrong* words. "Amanda and I are colleagues. I help her with the maintenance of the zoo, and she helps me with my research."

"How did she come to own a zoo?"

"It had to do with a couple of orphaned buffalo, a mountain lion and vacant land."

"Tell me about it."

"When Amanda's husband died about ten years ago, she inherited a large parcel of undeveloped acreage. He also left her his two pet buffalo and a scraggly old mountain lion who used to come by their house for food scraps."

"Pet buffalo?"

"I think he won them in a poker game. Anyway, Amanda tried to donate the buffalo to the Denver Zoo, but they didn't have room. She forgot about it for a while, just let things go. Then one of the buffalo was shot and killed. She never found out who did it. A nearsighted hunter, vandals, whoever. A few days later some of her neighbors decided that the mountain lion was dangerous. Amanda refused to allow them to hunt on her land. She told those people that animals on her property were protected, that she was declaring this land an independent zoological sanctuary."

They stopped in front of the large, flat enclosure. Four camels gazed through their long eyelashes. With haughty mien they munched their feed.

"Where'd the camels come from?" Nick asked. "Another poker game?"

"From a circus that disbanded. After Amanda declared herself a zoo and set up the legal parameters, the City Zoo began referring people with unwanted animals to her. And she began acquiring and trading. The camels, llamas and, of course, wapiti are well adapted to our climate."

"Of course," he remarked. "Wapiti?"

"American elk. Wapiti is the Indian name."

Taking people on a tour of the zoo was nothing new to Erica, and the familiarity of the ritual relaxed her until she dared to make a thorough study of her companion. The sun highlighted his sandy hair and vibrantly enhanced his tanned complexion. If the truth were told, she could have spent the day basking in the charmed physicality of his presence. Vaguely she noticed his lips moving. "Could you repeat that?"

"How many employees?"

She put her hormones on hold and answered by rote. "Amanda and I are the only full-time zookeepers, but there are two guys who do maintenance and a sweet night watchman named Tim. Plus over fifty part-time volunteers who Amanda coordinates to work as a regular zoo staff."

"Amanda must be quite an organizer."

"She's remarkable. She's managing quite an expensive operation on a shoestring budget."

Nick leaned against the split-rail fence that separated the camels from the walkway. "I'd like to see the monkeys," he said. "I mean, the chimps. *Pan troglodytes*, aren't they?"

Her eyes narrowed suspiciously. "It surprises me that you know the correct genus and species."

"Give me a chance, Erica. I'm not a complete imbecile."

As they followed a descending path through the zoo, Nick mentally patted himself on the back. The night before he'd done some reading on *Pan troglodytes*. They were part of the great ape family, native to the rain forests of equatorial Africa. Mostly they lived in tribes that were loosely governed by a dominant male. Their diet was primarily vegetarian. They reached sexual maturity at about age eight, and their life span could reach forty years.

He'd envisioned a similar encyclopedia entry for female zookeepers named Erica Swanson. Homo sapiens, female. She had a great little body with firm thighs and high breasts. Her eyes were dark and lively. Her curly dark brown hair begged to be touched. She was intelligent, feisty, unattached. And that, Nick thought, represented the sum of his data.

All the really important stuff required research. Like knowing her favorite color. And what she liked to eat. And what made her laugh.

She stopped beside a wood sign that read Primate Island. "Here we are."

He nodded. "Here we are."

Resting both hands on the smooth wooden fence, he peered across the wide moat. That clump of bushes and trees on the opposite side had to be the island, but he couldn't see anything moving. Apparently he wasn't the only one. Other spectators lined the fence and stared blankly into the foliage. Having scored points for reciting genus and species, Nick was reluctant to show his ignorance of the proper ape-watching procedure.

"There are four chimps," she said. "Two adults, male and female. The female has a one-year-old baby. And there's a juvenile male, close to Sheena's age."

"How big is the island?"

"About an acre, and it's almost a natural island, but we had to do some damming to divert the water flow on the opposite side. I've been here for about a year and a half, and the island has been my main project."

Eager to display his new knowledge, Nick added, "And the chimps don't escape because they're afraid of water."

"That's right."

Taking the cue from her steadfast gaze, he concentrated on the island. Nick had the disconcerting feeling that his minimal comprehension of chimp behavior sounded naive to her, as if he were making a pitiful attempt to please her. Ludicrous, he thought. He was a thirty-eight-year-old man. He didn't need to act like a schoolboy who was trying to impress the teacher.

"Actually the island isn't all that convenient," she said. "During the snowy winter months we spend a lot of time shuffling the chimps back and forth between here and an indoor enclosure."

He nodded, sneaking a glance at her profile. Her nose was small and cute, but well-defined eyebrows and thin lips gave her a serious demeanor. As far as he could tell, she was utterly without self-consciousness. Her curly hair was clean but unstyled. She wore no lipstick, no makeup at all. Was it possible, he wondered, that she didn't know how lovely she was?

"Look!" She gestured toward the island. "Here comes Java."

A chimp who looked much like Sheena ambled out from behind a shrub. He squatted, facing the giggling human observers, and very deliberately dissected a banana. Behind him a small pine tree trembled and shook.

"That must be Lenny," Erica said. "He's older, the dominant male. Poor Java has to put up with most of his aggressiveness."

A large chimp waddled forth. He gave three loud hoots, stood upright and hunched his shoulders. Walking slow and tough, he looked like a thug prepared for a rumble. The hair on his back and shoulders bristled in impressive display.

With a howl Java dropped his banana and scurried off, escaping into the boughs of a willow tree.

"Pushy old guy," Nick said.

"At the risk of assigning human values to chimps, I have to agree with you. Lenny's behavior is one reason I'm anxious to integrate Sheena into the tribe. If she was there, Java would have someone his own age to associate with. I think it might make a difference in developing his full dynamic potential."

"But Sheena doesn't want to stay?"

"I think it might be a matter of timing," Erica said. "It's only recently that Java has made a significant separation from his mother."

"His mother?"

"Oh, yes, Jenny and Lenny are Java's parents."

Nick took a harder look at the chimps. Father and son? Immediately he thought of several parallels between the apes and his own relationship with his son, Michael. "And you're studying bonding between Java and Lenny?"

"As it is specific to this situation. There's been a lot of work on primate bonding, some excellent long-standing studies by Goodall in Africa and through the Yale Institute."

Java crept down from the tree, baring his teeth and making low panting noises. His shuffling seemed submissive, almost apologetic. Finally he squatted beside Lenny and stretched out his hand. The larger chimp hooted, then patted his son's rump.

The other watchers laughed, but Nick felt a lump rise in his throat. The young chimp's approach seemed so forgiving, so needing of his father's attention. And Lenny had responded. It was like that with fathers and sons, he thought, a continual reaching out and rejecting. He swallowed hard before he spoke. "They really are a lot like us, aren't they?"

"Amazingly so. Genetically there's less than one percent difference between human DNA and that of chimps. They have long childhoods like we do, they learn from social situations and there's a similarity in our nonverbal behavior."

"Such as?"

"Hugging, petting and holding hands." As an illustration she ran her hand along his arm. "Stroking each other."

He caught her hand before she could withdraw it and raised her fingers to his lips. "Kissing?"

She nodded, trying to suppress her sudden exhilaration. Her physical attraction to him was truly incredible, impossible to ignore. Busily she retracted her hand, took a small spiral notebook from her back pocket and began scribbling. "It wasn't long ago that a direct confrontation with Lenny would have sent Java running to his mother."

There came a loud hoot-hoot from Lenny on the island. He stretched his long arms over his head and yawned. Java did the same. Then the two chimps knuckle-walked into their forest.

With disappointed groans the other human observers began to disperse. Nick turned his attention to Erica. "What are you writing down?"

"The time, the date and a brief description of this encounter." She dotted the last *i*, splotted the last period and closed her notebook. The exercise renewed her feeling of efficiency and control. "All right, Nick. What next?"

"Do you think the chimps will come back?"

"Sure, but it might not be for quite a while."

"Could we wait? I have to leave in about an hour, and I'd like to see them again."

She searched his expression for evidence of teasing, but no such attitude was evident. As far as she could tell, he was sincerely intrigued by the behavior of Java and Lenny.

"Since you have only an hour," she said, "we probably ought to finish our tour."

"May I come back another time?"

"Sure. Maybe you could help with the afternoon feeding."

Erica bit her lip. This was not an offer she made lightly. The care and feeding of her chimps were rigidly monitored. The introduction of a new caretaker meant a change in their environment. Why had she mentioned it? For one chilling moment she feared that her growing desire to spend more time with Nick had outweighed her dedication to research.

"I could feed them?" His voice was enthusiastic. "I'm tied up today, but how about tomorrow? Could I bring my son?"

"Absolutely not," she said with a firmness she didn't feel. "And you would only be allowed to observe. All right? No interacting with the chimps."

"I promise. You're the expert."

As they climbed the path and continued on their way around the park, Nick asked hundreds of questions about chimps and the bonding process. He barely glanced at the stately wapiti. His observation of the groundhog community was nonchalant. And he perfunctorily patted a reindeer, two buffalo and a braying donkey.

As they entered the small, cool Reptile House, his chimp mania waned slightly. "I never cared much for snakes, Erica."

"They're really quite pleasant and affectionate. Have you ever held one?"

"Never, and I don't intend to start now."

She dragged him over to a large glass cage containing two reticulated pythons. Each reptile was over four feet long. Their graceful bodies glided sinuously over the specially constructed branch in their cage. "These are Patty and Pete, the pythons. Come on, Nick. Aren't those markings beautiful?"

"Yeah, for a pair of shoes."

She laughed. "It may take some time, but I'm going to teach you to like snakes."

"I don't think I'll ever have the urge to cuddle up with a reptile. But, Erica, I will enjoy spending a long time with you."

His intimate tone gave her pause. "A long time" sounded vaguely as if he were looking toward a future, possibly a commitment. And she was as guilty as he was—making promises to teach him about reptiles and to let him go onto the island. Obviously she needed to clarify things before they went any further. "Nick, may I talk seriously with you?"

"Not here." He shuddered. "You might think they're cute, but I don't want to have snaky nightmares."

They walked into the sunlight, and Erica pointed toward a large, concrete outbuilding in the direction of Primate Island. "We'll go get Sheena."

"That's Sheena's place?" He whistled. "It's huge, a regular prefab Versailles."

"Actually it's the primate enclosure where they all live in winter. And there's also a kitchen."

"Great. I was wondering if maybe Sheena's reluctance to join the tribe has to do with a lack of bonding when she was young."

"Yes, I'm sure it does," she said dismissively. "Nick, there are a few things I feel we should discuss."

"Me, too. How old was Sheena when she was adopted by a human being? Is there a minimum bonding age for chimps?"

"If you don't mind, I'd rather not discuss the chimps."

"Okay." He matched her strides. "Well? What is it that you're so anxious to tell me?"

"I'm not anxious," she protested. Or was she?

"You sure look fidgety. The corner of your mouth is kind of pulled out of shape. Like a cute little fishhook."

"Stop teasing, Nick."

"All right." He arranged his features in a mockingly serious expression. "What's so important?"

"Us." She hadn't planned to make a bold statement, but his presumptions and her own burgeoning desire required a definition of terms. Where to start? "This is embarrassing."

"Maybe I can help," he said. "Would it be less difficult if I said I was very attracted to you?"

"Yes, that helps." Never before had she done anything like this. Despite her scientific orientation, Erica's relationships with men and her marriage had followed tradi-

tional patterns. The male did the asking, the structuring
of the relationship and the ultimate rejecting.

That was then, she told herself. This time she would be
clear about her wants; she would define the relationship
on her terms. These were new waters for Erica, but she
took a deep breath and leaped. "I think it would be wise
to outline the direction and the potential of our, um, acquaintance. You see, my career goals are extremely important to me."

He nodded. "I understand."

"Also, it might interest you to know that the physical
attraction between us is mutual." She cleared her throat.
Why did she sound like an old-maid schoolteacher? "My
suggestion is that—within certain restrictions—we allow
our natural biological urges to manifest themselves."

"Are you propositioning me, Erica?"

"The course I am suggesting might be construed as such,
that is, it could be..." Her voice trailed off as her gaze lifted
to his sensitive mouth. Such a handsome mouth. And his
golden-flecked eyes were so healthy and clear. Her common sense flew out the window, swift as a hummingbird
on the wing. "That's right, Nick. I'm propositioning you."

"I accept." He scanned the arid landscape of the zoo. "Is
there a handy bush we could hide behind to manifest our
urges? Or should we just do it right here in front of the
buffalo and the groundhogs and everybody?"

She averted her eyes. This wasn't what she'd wanted.
Her intention had been for a serious discussion. She paced
away from him into the shadow of Sheena's Versailles. "I'm
not explaining this well."

"Sure you are. It's a mating urge. Like with the chimps."

"Stop laughing at me, Nick."

"Believe me, lady. I'm not laughing."

She spun around and confronted him. "All right. Here's the deal. I have my life plotted out very carefully, and I am not in the market for any sort of permanent relationship."

"Fair enough."

"Right now I'm applying for grants to study primatology in Africa. I've been rejected by several places, but sooner or later somebody will come through. When I'm funded, I'll go. Nothing and no one will keep me here."

There, she'd said it. And she wondered why it was so vitally important to take this stand with Nick. He hadn't actually said he wanted permanence or a commitment. He hadn't even asked her on a date, for pity's sake. "Have I just made a perfect fool of myself?"

"Nobody's perfect."

"That's an old joke."

"Sorry, I couldn't resist. Actually, I appreciate your honesty."

She nodded. Honesty. That had been what she'd sought. A straightforward, honest, lustful relationship.

He reached toward her. His hand lightly traced the line of her high cheekbone, then drew away. "And I might even be able to help you."

"Help me?" Still feeling the delicate imprint of his touch, she shivered. Her biological attraction for him was reaching brain-boggling proportions. The anticipated climax would have to be stupendous. Fantastic. Incredible. But then she would have to walk away from him, bathed in incandescent independence.

"I have some connections with the Adventurers' Club," he continued. "And I know they give grants for research."

"The Adventurers' Club?"

"It's a bunch of rich old boys. And a couple of gals. They're eccentric but good-hearted. And they've been everywhere and done everything. They like to encourage other adventurers."

"But this isn't an adventure. It's research."

"For most of us mere mortals," he said dryly, "moving to a Third World country and setting up camp with a bunch of apes qualifies as adventure."

A surge of affection went through her. He was being more than understanding. Instead of making demands, he was on her side. She couldn't have hoped for a better response. Impulsively she took his face in her hands and placed a light kiss on the tip of his nose.

"Was that a thank-you?" he asked.

"It was."

"For fulfilling your life dream I get a peck on the nose?" In a swift movement he slipped his arms around her and pulled her close. "Let me show you a proper thank-you."

The firm pressure of his mouth was neither polite nor casual. It was breathtaking, all-consuming. The sensual promise of his lips demanded ardent response, and she abandoned herself to a wave of sensations. She tasted him, heard his breath within her. Behind her closed eyelids a brilliance exploded in wavering, fantastic designs. Her biological longing for him had finally been expressed. And she was not disappointed.

Her mouth fed greedily upon his, and she moaned when his tongue penetrated her lips. Her arms moved of their own volition to embrace him convulsively, cleaving his muscular torso against her breasts.

Shamelessly she rubbed against him, igniting a thrill that shimmered through her body. She was feverish with the heat of her desire. The tension in her lower abdomen was almost more than she could stand. And still he kissed her.

Her senses heightened to an almost painful acuity, and she could feel the separate imprint of each of his fingers on her back, embracing her flesh. Her heart pounded against his in a savage, primitive rhythm.

When the kiss ended, it took a moment for Erica to return to reality. Her gaze was unfocused, and she couldn't comprehend his sudden, awkward movements. "Nick, what are you doing?"

"I guess I'm not quite cured," he said as he rubbed vigorously at the back of his leg. "One of these animals activated my allergy."

He held out his arm, and she saw a patch of red pinpricklike spots that seemed to spread before her eyes. The backs of his legs behind his knees were also reddened.

"Oh, Nick, I'm so sorry. I wonder which one caused this." She gasped. "What if it's me?"

"Not to worry. I've never been allergic to women."

She was stung. Had there been many women? It was none of her business, but she was irritated at the thought. Had he tested his allergies against blondes and redheads?

He lifted his leg and scratched behind his knee. "I'm afraid I'd better get out of here, Erica. Besides, I'm already late for another appointment."

"Will I see you tonight?"

"Tomorrow."

Something crumpled inside her. Tomorrow? That was an eternity.

"There will be time for us, Erica."

"But—"

"Plenty of time."

He winked and hurried down the path toward the zoo's exit. As she gazed after him, Erica suspected that her brazen statement of independent lust had not entirely permeated his thick primate skull. He'd mentioned plenty of time. Hadn't she just told him she could be departing momentarily for Tanzania? Allergies or not, this retreat seemed awfully well-timed. As did his postponement of another meeting until tomorrow.

From a distance she studied his gait. He could have been Lenny the chimp, she thought. Despite Nick's occasional pauses to scratch, he had the unmistakable swagger of a dominant male.

Erica cocked her head. He'd better not be planning to manipulate their impending relationship. He might be naturally dominant, but she could be very determined.

This time Erica vowed that she would be calling the shots.

3

AT HIGH NOON on the following day Nick stretched across his desk at Barron's Amusement Park and handed her a clipboard.

"What's this for?"

"In case you need to make notes."

Erica was stiff as a rake. The oath she'd made less than twenty-four hours earlier—her personal vow to control the development of their relationship—had been severely undermined.

"Let me get this straight," she said. "In your humble opinion, I will need a clipboard to record the pearls of wisdom that drop from your lips."

"I couldn't have put it better myself."

She tossed the clipboard onto the desk. "I'll manage with memory alone."

"Before we get started, would you care for lunch?"

"No, thank you." She couldn't help adding, "I prefer healthier food than hot dogs and ice cream."

"I was thinking of the Gazebo Restaurant. I don't run that particular concession, but the chef is a personal friend. I could request a bean sprout sandwich for you."

"Not necessary. I'd rather get this over with as quickly as possible so I can return to my work at the zoo."

He led her through the door of his office. "I take it you don't approve of Amanda's plan for you to spend the day with me, studying the layout of Barron's."

"Indeed, I don't."

"Erica?" When he touched her elbow, she spun around to face him. The bright yellow jersey of her sundress whispered against his thighs. He wanted to kiss her, to soothe the red flush in her tanned cheeks, to tell her she was beautiful when she was angry. But he knew a comment like that was asking for a megaton explosion.

"Yes, Nick? Was there something you wanted to say? Should I prepare to make a mental note?"

"I like your dress."

"Thank you," she snapped, more irritated with herself than at him. No one had forced her to change her clothes after leaving the zoo. Of her own accord she'd slipped into the scooped-neck, sleeveless sundress that flattered her slim waist and flared becomingly at her knees. Had she unconsciously absorbed some of Amanda's romantic ideas? "Let's get on with the tour, shall we?"

"Fine with me. We'll go for an overview." He directed her toward the Ferris wheel. "You're not afraid of heights, are you?"

"I'm not afraid of anything."

He tried a warm, friendly grin. It was met with a glare of such icy intensity he could practically feel his lips turning blue. For the sake of self-preservation he looked away.

They joined a short line in front of the colorful vertical wheel and inched forward in silence. In a swift proprietary glance he determined that the ride was clean. The red enameled hearts and golden curlicues that decorated the spokes and the two-person chairs gleamed in the sunlight. Likewise the operator of the ride was neatly groomed in his bright blue Barron's T-shirt.

Nick shifted his gaze to the landscaped midway. Family groups strolled past a bright strip of geraniums and a sculpted hillside display of pines and tiger lilies. A nice-size crowd, he thought, enough people to create a sense of motion, but few enough that they weren't bumping into one another. Nick was satisfied... satisfied with the flowers, the attendance and the Ferris wheel. Erica's attitude was another matter.

Sure, he'd expected her to be annoyed, but he wasn't prepared for an outing with Attila the Hun. Why couldn't she relax? He sincerely wanted what was best for her. And best for him. For both of them.

It wasn't until they were latched into the chair that Nick offered an observation. "You're snarling."

"Am I?" She scrunched over to the far side of the seat, too infuriated even to want accidental physical contact with him. Amanda's plan was a blatant foray into romantic matchmaking. Worse than that! "Maybe I'm annoyed because I don't appreciate the fact that you and Amanda conspired behind my back."

"Now it's a conspiracy."

"Besides which, I need to spend time with the chimps every day. This so-called plan shows a total disregard for my work."

When she'd reported at the zoo that morning, Amanda had preempted her schedule. Playing Cupid, she'd insisted that Erica spend the day with Nick at Barron's—studying his promotional techniques with an eye to incorporating his expertise into the arrangement of Golden Independent Zoo.

The Ferris wheel jolted higher and higher, gradually taking on a load of passengers.

"This isn't entirely Amanda's fault," he said.

"I didn't presume that it was."

"But it wasn't all my idea, either." He shifted his weight and the seat swung gently. "Anyway, after you talked to me yesterday about manifesting our natural urges, I figured you might enjoy spending the day together."

"Did you? And why didn't you ask me directly? Instead of cooking up this lame excuse for a rendezvous."

"Amanda's plan isn't without merit," he argued. "When I telephoned to thank her for the tour, she told me the zoo needed cash flow. She wants to encourage heavier attendance."

"That's true. But I'm not the most qualified person to send on this mission. I'm a primatologist, not a publicist."

"You're a student of behavioral patterns, right?"

"Basically."

"And that's exactly what you're doing here," he concluded. "Studying behavior."

They had reached the pinnacle of the Ferris wheel's arc, two stories above the park. Erica leaned forward, scanning the grounds and causing their seat to rock gently. She enjoyed the motion; being suspended in space tickled her.

"Look to your right." He pointed. "There's the entry with miniature golf courses. Through the Russian olive trees you can see the top of the carousel. That's also where Kiddy Land is. To your left is the roller coaster. The Gazebo Restaurant is behind us. Band shell and lily pond are dead ahead."

"How much land do you have?"

"Thirty acres, not including the parking lot. And there's a significant point. If you want crowds, you need a big parking lot. Convenience is important."

The Ferris wheel ride started again, and with a whoosh they descended.

Erica gasped with pleasure. As they climbed again to the heights, she sucked in her cheeks, trying to look severe, but the fun of this arcing ride defeated her composure and she giggled. "It's been a hundred years since I've done this."

"Obviously too long."

They swooped again, and she let go with a laugh. It felt as if she were floating. "Too long for what?"

"Being swept off your feet."

She speared him with a sidelong glance. "You're pretty damn sure of yourself, aren't you?"

"That I am." They circled again. "And I love to take Ferris wheel rides with a pretty woman."

"Thank you." His compliment, no matter how off-hand, gratified her. It had been a long time, a very long time, since a man had told her she was attractive.

The Ferris wheel whisked them through sunlit space. She felt pretty.

After another floating descent her anger was almost gone. Though she still didn't like the idea that he and Amanda had taken a decision out of her hands, she could live with it.

Nick signaled to the operator of the ride, and he and Erica were the first to alight.

"Well, are we having fun yet?"

"That was fun," she admitted. They moved out of the stream of traffic and stood in the shade of a pine. "Listen, Nick, I don't want to spend the whole day being peeved, but I want you to understand that I hate being manipulated. Don't ever do it again."

"You've got it. From this moment forward I promise to be direct."

She held out her hand. "Shake on it?"

"Let's not get formal."

Instead of shaking, he clasped her hand in his, and they strolled along a cobblestoned path that meandered away from the stand of pines to a shady grove of leafy catalpa trees. Though the sound and presence of other people were all around them, the artful landscaping created a sense of seclusion.

This is nice, she thought, *very nice*. The cool green shade of the trees. The trickling splash of a fountain. The pleasant familiarity of his hand in hers. Being swept off her feet might not be such a horrendous fate.

"So, Erica, how long since you've been to an amusement park?"

"Not since high school. To a carnival that was passing through our area."

"No Disney World? No Sea World?"

"No way. With seven kids in the family that kind of vacation was out of the question. Not only would it be too costly, but the logistics were like mobilizing a platoon. I remember one trip we took from our home in Whitworth, Wisconsin, to St. Louis. Nine sweaty bodies packed into a van like sardines. I almost dismembered my younger sister, Elise."

She shook her head with a mixture of fondness and regret. To be sure, she loved all the members of her large family. Yet it was difficult being in the middle—too young to be part of the grown-up schemes of the elder siblings and too old to enjoy baby games. Erica had spent much of her youth lost in daydreams. First she'd fantasized fairy tales, then she'd mentally escaped to an exotic wonderland featuring primatology studies in Africa.

Wistfully she recalled those youthful daydreams and the freedom of those fantasies. In her fantasies nothing had been impossible. She remembered summer afternoons perched in the oak tree behind the barn as she thumbed through her precious, dog-eared *National Geographic* magazines.

Nick interrupted her reverie. "What do your folks do?"

"They own a dairy farm. Once Dad experimented with an ice-cream manufacturing plant. Hence, my lifelong disgust for frozen, sugared-up milk."

"It didn't work out?"

Ruefully she shook her head. "It never seemed to work out. Dad always had grandiose plans for making a million dollars, and all of them fell flat."

He'd had good intentions. And great enthusiasm. She couldn't help laughing when she told Nick about the time she'd caught her father's entrepreneurial spirit and devised the Swanson International Petting Zoo.

With her dad's encouragement she'd posted handmade signs along the road. Unfortunately their roadways were only traveled by other farmers, who were not terribly excited about the stellar opportunity to pet a cow and have four piglets eat corncobs from their hands.

"I remember another time," she confided, "when Dad used the livestock as collateral to finance a gold-mining operation."

"In Wisconsin?"

"It didn't exactly—pardon the pun—'pan' out. That was the only time Mom got seriously angry at him. She was furious, slamming around the kitchen like a tornado. And his only reassurance was to tell her over and over— 'Nothing to worry about. No banker in his right mind is going to repossess cows.'"

"Your Dad sounds like an interesting guy."

"Dreamers usually are. They're exciting and popular. Not awfully well respected, but very, very interesting."

She couldn't help the twinge of bitterness she felt when she thought of the consequences of having a dreamer for a father. Obtaining her education had been a financial struggle, and she was still fighting to raise enough money for further research. If only Dad had managed their resources more sensibly. If only Mom hadn't reproduced every other year. If. If. If.

"I love them all dearly," she said. "But there were so many of us. Sometimes I can't help wishing that we'd been a more normal family."

"I know what you mean. I hated being known as 'the boy who lives at Barron's.' I never knew if the other kids liked me for myself or because coming over to my house meant free rides and refreshments."

They stopped beside the lily pond. Though a crowd strolled on the arched red bridge, the large pond carpeted with round leaves and white flowers gave an impression of serenity.

"Do you have brothers and sisters, Nick?"

"One younger sister. She lives in California and has a family. My mother is out visiting her this summer. My father burned out early. He died two years ago."

"I'm sorry."

She noticed a flicker of emotion behind his eyes before he replied. "I'm sorry, too. My father and I were always at each other's throats. Always fighting. He wanted me to stay here and run the family business. But I wasn't ready. Not until now."

"Then you haven't always worked at Barron's?"

"Nope." He gave her a wry grin. "I might look like I was born wearing an organ-grinder costume, but I've only been here for the past two years."

"And what did you do before? No, wait. Let me guess. You seem like a casual, laid-back guy, but I'll bet you're athletic. Were you a golf pro?"

"When I play, which isn't often, tennis is my game."

"Maybe a teacher? Or a coach?"

He shook his head.

She wrinkled her nose and considered. It was difficult to imagine him in a profession that required wearing a suit. "Something in the arts? A writer? An actor?"

"*Moi*? You've got to be joking."

"Maybe you were a shopkeeper. Or owned a restaurant. That's it. You ran a restaurant specializing in soda pop and junk food."

"Not even close. I was a stockbroker in New York."

"You?" She couldn't believe it. "You wore a pin-striped suit and worked on Wall Street?"

"Lady, I was tailored right down to my Guccis, had an apartment with a view in Manhattan and a house in Connecticut. I worked twelve-hour days, went to three-martini lunches and handled millions of dollars in investments daily."

She was amazed. "I never would have guessed."

"That's a compliment. I've tried really hard to leave that behind me."

"Why?" It sounded to Erica like an exotic, glamorous life.

"I'd rather be who I am today. Don't get me wrong. I don't regret my past. Wall Street provided me with a good living. I've done everything I've wanted to do, traveled to wherever I wanted to go. But a couple of years ago something changed in me. I used to crave tension, needed it to feel alive. Not anymore. Barron's is enough for me. As you noticed, I'm a settled-down, laid-back kind of guy. What about you?"

"The opposite. So far, my life has been all preparation."

"For what?"

"Field study in Africa. When I have my grant, my life will really begin."

"What if something happens before that?" He started walking again and tossed off his next comment with studied carelessness. "Like falling in love, getting married, having babies."

"That won't happen, Nick."

He directed her off the beaten path, rustling through the knee-high pussy willows that bordered the pond. Beneath a drooping willow tree, Nick kicked off his loafers and rolled up his denim jeans. He gave her a one-word explanation. "Litter."

In the placid water she spied two red-and-white striped popcorn boxes. Nick waded out a few feet and grabbed the soggy cardboard. He was back beside her in a moment. "I hate litter. I've got eight employees who do nothing but pick up trash, and they're busy all day long."

"We have the same problem at the zoo, and we don't even have concession stands."

"You don't?" He jammed his feet into his shoes. "Why not? Is it a danger to the animals?"

"It could be. But most people respect the signs. Don't Feed the Animals."

They headed back toward the main walkway. "Food isn't prohibited on the grounds?"

"It's not encouraged, but we have picnic areas."

"A refreshment stand is something Amanda should consider." He went to a trash container and deposited the offending litter. "Food concessions are very profitable."

She gritted her teeth to keep from growling. Thus far he'd made two suggestions—food stands and parking lots. Both were repulsive. In fact, the whole idea of recruiting more visitors to the zoo was fairly objectionable. Erica preferred an unobtrusive clientele who didn't interfere with her research.

As they crossed the red bridge, Nick read her expression. "Oh, no, Erica the Red returns. You look like you're ready to lead a ravaging horde."

She gave a teasing snarl.

"Don't get me wrong," Nick said. "It's a fearsome look. Your eyebrows pull down into this mean, straight line. And your upper lip kind of twitches. Do chimps make faces like that?"

She remembered Sheena bashing her monkey doll. "They have ways of making their displeasure known."

"Show me."

"Not here in front of all these people."

He continued to tease as they followed the sound of guitars and folksingers to the Oriental-looking bandstand, which was surrounded by bonsai trees and lava rocks. In the shade of an elm they found a vacant bench. "Come on, Erica. Just do one little chimp thing for me."

She relented. "Give me your arm."

He did. "You will notice that there is no rash. I'm experimenting with a new allergy treatment."

She laid his arm across her lap and began inspecting it. Then she combed through the fine, dark hair with her fingernails. "This is how chimps relax," she said. "It's called grooming. I don't suppose you have lice?"

"I hope not."

They sat quietly, listening to the soft music of folksingers and guitars. Strangely, Erica found the chimpish gestures calming. Touching him had a soothing effect on her. It was talking to him that got her back up. They could have a marvelous relationship, she thought, if she could convince him to keep his mouth shut.

"It is relaxing," he said. "I like it."

"You would." She grinned. "Grooming is particularly effective on the lower forms of primate."

"Speaking of which . . ." He waved to a young man who was wearing a red Barron's T-shirt. "That's my son, Michael."

"Nice-looking boy," she said as the tall, blond youth approached the bench where they were sitting.

"Of course he is. Takes after his father."

She snickered.

"That's true, isn't it? A biological fact. Good-looking parents produce good-looking offspring."

"Nick, old man, it ain't necessarily so."

When he introduced her to his son, Erica realized how very much the sixteen-year-old boy resembled his father. Same golden eyes, same strong features, same charming smile. Only Michael was two inches taller and his hair was much lighter than Nick's sandy brown.

Michael flashed the Barron smile. "Pleased to meet you."

"Thank you, Michael. It's nice to meet you, too."

As Nick observed their handshake, he was overcome by a strong emotion, but he couldn't quite identify the feeling. A sense of fulfillment? There was something very, very right about this moment. Though short, dark-haired Erica and his Nordic son were physically as opposite as two people could be, they looked natural together. But that wasn't quite it, he realized. His presence was necessary to complete the picture. Together they looked like a family.

Offhandedly Michael said, "So you must be the lady with the chimps. Sheena's mother?"

"Oh, dear, I hope not."

Nick quickly stepped in, anxious to defuse any possible conflict. "She knows what you mean."

"Of course I do," she said. "I was just thinking about how my mother used to complain when people called her 'Erica's mother' or 'Eddie's mom.' Now I guess I know how she felt."

Nick's laughter was too loud, but his sense of satisfaction had overwhelmed his usual poise. He had made a quantum leap to a conclusion. They could be a family. From the first time he'd seen Erica, he'd known there was something special about their connection. That was why he'd refused to see her the previous evening. He didn't want to follow up on her proposition that they mindlessly mate, because he wanted a future with her, not a casual affair. In Erica he saw a woman who could share with him, become a part of his life and complete his family.

"Hey, Dad. Wake up. I asked if you were the one who chose the band's music today." He turned to Erica. "My Dad gets real weird about sixties' guitars and folksingers."

"No kidding." She cast a devilish grin toward Nick. "The oldies but goodies, huh?"

Michael laughed. "Do you like that stuff, Miss Swanson?"

"Call me 'Erica,' and no, I don't. I like hard rock, played really loud. But, of course, I do like some of the oldies—the Dead and the Stones and even sometimes the Beatles. But loud. Probably because I don't often get to listen to loud music. It bothers the animals."

"Which shows that animals have good sense," Nick said. "And what do you mean by 'oldie but goodie'?"

"Elevator music," she said.

As the trio with guitars ended a gentle rendition of "Where Have All the Flowers Gone?" Nick strode toward the bandstand. "I'll show you elevator music?"

Erica and Michael watched as Nick called the band to the edge of the stage for a brief consultation.

"What do you suppose he's doing?" Erica asked.

"You never know. My dad's a real wild guy, you know." He leaned toward her. "So how many apes have you got at this zoo?"

"Four on Primate Island. And Sheena."

"That's cool. I used to have this old dog when I lived with my mom." He shuffled his feet. "Sometimes I miss pets."

The three guitarists had abandoned their acoustic instruments and plugged in electric guitars. The onstage microphones buzzed, and electronic amplifiers whined to life.

Erica chuckled when the band launched into a driving rendition of Elvis Presley's greatest rock 'n' roll hits. As Nick turned toward her, he transformed himself into a sixties' greaser by rolling up the sleeves of his shirt and pulling a strand of his sandy hair into an imitation of an Elvis spit curl. He stuck a pair of dark sunglasses on his nose and moved his feet in a shuffle that was remotely similar to Chuck Berry's duck walk.

Erica rolled her eyes and laughed. "Michael, your father is absolutely nuts."

"I told you so. Hey, I didn't mean to insult you—when I said you were Sheena's mother."

"It's okay, Michael. I know you didn't."

"It was kind of a label, you know? Like a way I could tell you from the others."

The others? "Are there so many?"

"Oh, yeah, Dad's a real man-about-town."

When she looked up at him, Michael turned away. He hunched his shoulders and furrowed his eyebrows as he focused his full attention on the toe of his hightop sneaker. If he'd been a chimp, she would have defined his expression as defensive—tentatively reaching out but fearful of being hurt. "Michael? Is there something you want to tell me?"

"I don't know."

From her vast experience with a mob of brothers and sisters, she knew better than to push. Instead she turned back toward the blasting sounds of rock 'n' roll.

Several teenagers had been drawn toward the throbbing beat from the bandstand. They bobbed up and down like corks in a water bucket. An attractive redheaded girl was dancing her way toward Michael, but he was too busy staring at his shoes to notice. Then he blurted out, "That's a lie, what I said before. My dad hardly ever dates. He's real settled down, real tied down."

"Does that bother you?"

"Yeah. No. Well, sometimes I think he does it because of me, you know, and I don't want him to. It seems like he tries to stay home so I won't be alone."

"Are you lonesome?"

"Hey, I'm okay. I don't want to talk about it, you know?"

"Yes," she said softly. "I know."

Nick managed to wend his way through the dancers and back to them. He whirled in a circle and whipped off his sunglasses. "Do you call that elevator music?"

Erica rolled her eyes. "You old swinger, you."

Nick threw his arm around her shoulder. "Come on, Michael. Let's buy this lady a glass of water."

"That's okay, Dad. You two go ahead." As he joined the crowd of dancing teens, he said over his shoulder, "Nice to meet you, Erica."

"Same here."

Linking arms with Nick, she glanced one last time toward his son. Their exchange had bothered her. She knew what it was to be lonely, and it must be worse for Michael because he didn't even have animal companions. "Michael seemed very interested in the chimps."

"He loves animals. That's one reason I want to get rid of this allergy. Michael would like to have a pet."

She detached herself from Nick and went to his son. "Michael, would you like to come out to the zoo on Saturday? You could help me feed the chimps."

She was rewarded with a genuine smile. "You bet."

"See you then."

She returned to Nick, who had watched the exchange with a puzzled expression. "What was that all about?"

"Since your allergies prevent you from helping out on Primate Island, I've recruited your son."

Never mind that she made a practice of discouraging other people from associating with her chimps. Never mind that she didn't have time to spend with a lonely teenage boy. Never mind that her relationship with Nick seemed to be getting more complicated by the minute. Erica felt good about her plans for young Michael.

Nick ruffled her hair affectionately. "You really aren't afraid of anything. Not many women would take on both of the notorious Barron men."

"I can handle it."

She fell into step beside him, and they strolled away from the music, through the gardens and past a man-made waterfall. Erica's thoughts drifted gently toward plans for the evening. An evening alone with Nick. Surely Amanda would agree to "chimp-sit" Sheena.

She stopped beside the waterfall and held out her hand, catching the shimmering droplets. Tonight might be wonderful.

"By the way," Nick said, "I checked into grant possibilities from the Adventurers' Club. And they just happen to have a fund for encouraging adventures. Over half a million dollars sitting in a bank account, gathering interest."

Erica's heart stopped. She hadn't really taken the Adventurers' Club seriously. "You're kidding."

"When I mentioned that you were a primatologist who wanted to set up camp in Africa, they were enthusiastic."

Her heartbeat revved. She couldn't believe it. Her plans, her hopes and dreams were possible. They could all come true.

"There're only a couple of things you need to do to qualify," he said. "They want to meet you and ask a few questions. And they want a formal presentation."

"Like a speech?"

"And maybe a few slides," he suggested.

"Nick, do you really think they're serious?"

"They're for real. The guy I talked to mentioned that in return for their grant monies, you'd be expected to hit the lecture circuit once a year for three years. And maybe to write a book."

Erica wasn't surprised. Lectures and publication were an almost inevitable part of fund-raising. Excitedly she bobbed her head.

"Here's the bad news. They want this presentation at their regular monthly meeting on Friday. That's tomorrow night."

"Tomorrow?" Her eyes went wide with terror. The chance to do an actual presentation was the closest she'd been to acceptance. But she certainly wasn't prepared to speak. "I'll blow it. I can't do it tomorrow."

"Sure you can." He breezily encouraged her. "Don't you have some slides from your trips to Africa?"

"Well, yes. Some from Goodall's camp. And a couple of others of the chimps at the zoo." Her panic was rising. "But tomorrow? Nothing is organized for a presentation. My slides are dusty—they live in a box in the bottom drawer of my dresser."

"Erica, you're dithering."

"Dithering? Dithering?"

"Select a few slides and talk about them."

"This isn't a home movie show, Nick ... My Summer at the Gombe River. I'm asking these people for a lot of money. I can't waltz in there unprepared."

"I thought you weren't afraid of anything."

Except for failing. "What if I can't get it all together? Isn't there another time?"

He took both her hands in his. "You'll do great. You're a smart, poised lady who has a lot of knowledge. I believe in you, Erica. One hundred percent."

For an instant her fear subsided. His touch gentled her. In his gold-flecked eyes she could see brilliant reflections of the most wonderful possibilities in the world. Maybe everything would work out the way she wanted. Maybe her presentation would be superb. Oh, sure, and maybe chimps could fly. "Why didn't you tell me about this as soon as you heard?"

"I didn't think there'd be a problem."

"You're right. There shouldn't be. I should have anticipated this sort of thing. Now it's all screwed up."

"Don't underestimate yourself, Erica. You can do it."

She lowered her gaze, reviewing her past failures, from the Swanson International Petting Zoo to her divorce to all the rejections from other grant foundations. Her arms went limp as a measure of determination drained from her. Was she reaching too high? Wanting too much?

Quietly he repeated, "You can do it, Erica."

"Oh, sure, you can be calm. You're not giving a slide show tomorrow night. Your future doesn't depend on doing well."

"Good," he said.

"What do you mean 'good'? I'm a basket case, and you're nodding and saying it's good?"

"You're feisty again. For two seconds you looked like a whipped puppy. Now you're ready to take on the world."

He was absolutely right. She wasn't going to roll over and give up without trying. Not now. Not ever. When he squeezed her hands, she responded with renewed strength. She still felt pressured, but not overwhelmed. "I haven't even thanked you."

"You're welcome."

Remembering the last time he'd explained a proper thank-you, she drew away quickly. If she was going to be ready for a slide show tomorrow night, she needed to spend tonight preparing. "I'd better hustle myself home and get organized."

"Is there anything I can do to help?"

"Yes. No."

"And what does that mean?"

The "yes" was wishful thinking. She wanted to fulfill her constantly postponed fantasy of a night with him. The "no" was reality. She cleared her throat and said, "I've got a lot of work to do."

"I could hold your hand," he offered. "Wipe your fevered brow. Make dinner. Ice the water."

She was tempted.

He continued. "I could turn down the covers on the bed, pop the cork on the champagne. Do you like oysters?"

She backed away from him, trying futilely to create enough physical distance to overcome her desire. "Putting together a presentation is going to take concentration, and I have the feeling that you, Nick Barron, would be too much of a distraction."

4

"AND SO, ladies and gentlemen of the Adventurers' Club, because of my unique qualifications—a) field experience in observing the behavior of higher primates and b) my ongoing primatological studies within the confines of a zoo—I would be very grateful if you should decide to accept my proposal."

Erica scowled at her reflection in the bathroom mirror. What a wimpish conclusion! She cleared her throat and tried a more strident finish. "I demand that you fund me."

She wrinkled her nose. Now she sounded less like an anthropologist and more like a terrorist.

"I humbly demand and request . . ." Too confused.

"I beg you . . ." Yuck, too pathetic.

She spun on her heel and marched out of the bathroom. Her marathon of organizing slides and working on her presentation was almost over. Only two hours and twenty minutes until the meeting at the Adventurers' Club.

Her preparations had been frustrating when she couldn't put her hands on precisely the slide she wanted and gratifying when she realized how much knowledge she actually had amassed in her years of study.

"'Give me money,'" she sang. Now she was definitely getting silly. Time for a break.

In her bedroom she checked the blue silk dress and matching jacket she planned to wear to the meeting. The buttons were all intact. The hem was even. The shirtwaist dress was unwrinkled and neat. Very good. Though she'd already showered and combed her curly chestnut hair into as much of a style as possible, she would wait until the last minute before changing out of her tank top and cutoffs.

Her wristwatch indicated two hours and fifteen minutes until Nick would arrive to pick her up for the meeting. What could she do to relax? Sleep was out of the question. She was much too tense. Likewise for reading a book. She searched through her selection of tapes until her fingers came to rest on "Sgt. Pepper's Lonely Hearts Club Band" by the Beatles. An oldie but goodie. Though it wasn't Elvis Presley, "Sgt. Pepper" was music both she and Nick might enjoy.

She shook her head and sighed. Nick Barron. Where was he at this very moment? Dressed up in a crazy costume? Riding on a Ferris wheel? Fishing litter from the lily pond? Because of Nick she had this wonderful, nerve-racking opportunity to present her proposal for funding. Because of the opportunity, however, the rapid progress of their acquaintance had screeched to a halt. Of course, that didn't mean that it couldn't start up again with few preliminaries. Very soon, she told herself, there would be a time for them, a time when she could give into the sensual feelings he so easily aroused in her.

She took the "Sgt. Pepper" tape into the front room and popped it into her tape deck. This would be a rare treat— playing her music loudly without headphones. When Sheena was here, Erica always kept the volume low. But Sheena was at the zoo, having spent last night and all of today with Amanda.

Though Erica missed the little beast, the solitude had been marvelous. Having her own space, a room of her own, had been a constant problem in her life. Just as Nick complained about growing up under a roller coaster, she'd been surrounded with six siblings. Another thing they had in common? Yes, she decided, both of them appreciated the need for space. But, of course, they'd chosen to deal with it in different ways. While Nick liked the silence of a heavily soundproofed room, Erica preferred to drown out distractions with loud, mind-numbing rock 'n' roll.

She bopped into the kitchen in time to the beat and peered into the refrigerator. Might be wise to eat something, but the idea of fruit salad again was so unappealing that her stomach did a flip-flop. Nervous? Erica held up her hand, noticing a slight tremor in the index finger. Yes, she was nervous. Who wouldn't be? Her future, her career, her dreams rested on this presentation.

She sang her own lyrics to the music on the tape. "Unaccustomed as I am to public speaking, I will do all right, oh, yeah, all right."

If she didn't, it wasn't the end of the world. There would be other opportunities if she blew this one, but the funding process was so horribly slow. She could almost hear the time ticking away, second by second. Thud. Thud. Thud. Was there someone at the door? Erica ran to answer the door.

"Hi, Nick. You're early." She burst into a wide smile. Nick would help her pass these last dragging moments. Remembering yesterday, she knew that he could comfort her. It was just as likely, however, that he would choose to drive her crazy or tease her into apoplexy.

"I've been hammering on this door for three minutes." He winced at the noise as he entered her apartment.

"I told you that I like loud music," she shouted.

"This loud?" he shouted back, then turned down the volume on her tape player and shook his head. "How can you hear yourself think? You and my son ought to get along very well."

"I like Michael. He seems like a good kid, and I'm glad he's coming to the zoo with me tomorrow." Again it seemed that she was babbling. Dithering, as Nick had called it. But she couldn't stop herself. She felt as if she were poised on the edge of a cliff, waiting for the wind to change before she tested her fragile wings. "Michael does seem a bit lonely, Nick. Does he ever see his mother?"

"Frequently. He spends holidays with her in California, but he's been living with me for the past year and a half."

"Then he joined you after you left your Wall Street job in New York."

"My former life-style was a lousy environment for a kid. I was always working, and when I came home, I was wiped out." He shrugged. "You would probably be the first to tell me that for a growing boy like Michael, Manhattan is not a natural habitat."

"Ah, yes," she teasingly concurred. "Environment is important to this bonding process. By the way, you're early, aren't you? You're not going to spring something on me—like we have to be there in ten minutes?"

"Are you ready to make your speech?"

"Yes." She gestured to her box of slides, projector and a thick sheaf of notes on yellow, legal-size paper. "I did, however, plan to spend these last few hours pacing and generally having hysterics."

"Are you nervous?"

Again she held out her hand. The slight tremor had accelerated to a full-fledged flutter. She wasn't sure whether that was entirely due to prepresentation jitters or the sensual tremors she always experienced in Nick's presence. "You might say that I'm a little tense."

When his gaze swept over her body and focused just below her cleavage, Erica looked down. She wasn't wearing a bra, and—much to her embarrassment—her taut nipples pushed against the thin material of her tank top. She couldn't decide whether to fold her arms over her breasts or ignore the situation. Flustered, she whirled away from him and marched into the kitchen. "Are you hungry?"

"I know something that might relax you, Erica."

"How about dinner?"

"How about a massage?"

Oh, sure. Erica knew her self-control would vanish if she allowed him to touch her. As pleasant and wonderful as a massage sounded, she was not about to add that sort of encounter to her already frenzied state of mind. "Maybe you should leave, Nick. Come back in an hour, after I'm dressed for the meeting."

"Why not a comfortable massage right now?" he persisted. "You're not scared of me, are you?"

"Don't even try that game with me. I grew up with a mob of brothers and sisters, remember? I'm familiar with dare and double-dare. The last time I fell for that, I was ten and I ended up on crutches for two weeks."

"Double-dare?" His expression was mockingly innocent. "I must have forgotten how it works. Tell me about it."

"Oh, sure, you've forgotten."

"Hey, I only had one sister, and she was a sissy."

She eyed him suspiciously. "Okay. Here's how a dare works. A long time ago my brother Eddie and I were up in the second story of the barn. It was the end of summer, and we were swinging out on a rope and dropping about six feet into a mountainous truckload of hay. Eddie said, 'Anybody can jump from here, but it takes guts to do it off the roof of the barn.' He dared me. Then I was dumb enough to double-dare him."

"Why was that dumb?"

"Double-dares go first. That's the code. If I hadn't jumped, I would have been branded a coward forever." Her lips curved in a wry grin. "Actually that would have been a better fate than spraining my ankle."

"You're smiling."

"Eddie broke his wrist. When I look back on it, he was even dumber than I was. He saw what happened to me, and he jumped, anyway. The point to this story is that I've learned to look before I leap."

"Erica, I'm not talking about a plummet through thin air. All I mentioned was a massage to relax you. What can that hurt?"

Though she wouldn't sprain her ankle, Erica feared the possible consequences of having him so near, caressing her body. On the other hand, she wasn't ten anymore. She could control herself. Wasn't that what she'd vowed? To control the course of this relationship.

"Okay, Nick. You're on."

"A flat surface is preferable for massage," he said after a glance at the grass mats on the floor of the living room. "The bedroom?"

She groaned inwardly. "Sure, why not?"

After escorting him to her inner sanctum, she carefully stretched out on the primrose coverlet on her four-poster bed.

"Nice room," he said. "Very feminine."

"Let's get this over with, Nick."

"It's not going to hurt. I promise." He sat beside her on the bed and ran his fingertip along her spine. She quivered beneath his touch.

Nick gazed down on her prone body. The thin material of her tank top molded the shape of her neck, and her cut-off Levi's stretched snugly over her hips. Her tan line was unusual. Because, he supposed, she was usually dressed

the shorts and shirt of her zoo uniform, her tan was
arker on her lower arms and legs. It faded up her shoul-
ers to a pale ivory at her nape.

She fidgeted into a comfortable position. "I'm ready."

"So am I," he murmured, admiring the tapering line of
er torso and the roundness of her firm buttocks. Though
ension knotted her muscles, his impression was of soft-
ess and a delicate bone structure. Beneath her strength,
e sensed a lovely, sweet vulnerability.

Lightly he placed his hands on either side of her waist
with his thumbs toward her spine. His fingers ascended her
ack, kneading gently, until he reached her nape. There
is efforts were more strenuous. "Relax, Erica."

She groaned. "I'm trying."

"Your upper back feels like steel." He held her shoul-
ers and lowered his head to within a few inches of her
ace. "You're not breathing," he accused.

"Of course I'm breathing," she snapped. "I'd die if I
wasn't breathing."

"Deep breaths," he instructed.

He watched her rib cage expand with the first deep in-
alation, and the movement struck a chord of excitement
within him. She exhaled and her torso slimmed. "Again,"
e instructed.

She did as he told her, and again he marveled at the
imple breath-taking process. He also thoroughly en-
oyed her physical response to his commands. "Again."

Inhale. Exhale. He breathed in rhythm with her.
Again."

"Nick, I don't want to hyperventilate."

"One more time."

She took a deep shuddering breath and expelled it.

"Wow," he said.

"Wow what?"

"That's a great little motion you've got there. Kind of
tremble across the shoulder blades and all the way dow
to your bottom."

"Don't be silly. I'm just breathing."

"I know."

His hands rested on her back, absorbing her, feeling th
life within her. His fascination with her had expanded
such idiotic, immense proportions that her every brea
fueled his incipient arousal. He truly hadn't come to h
apartment intending to make love to her. His early a
rival was motivated by a desire to help, to see if there w
anything he could do to help, and he knew this wasn't a
appropriate time for their mutual seduction. He kne
that.

"Nick?" She turned and propped herself on one elbo
to look up at him. "What happened to the massage?"

"You really don't know, do you?"

"Don't know what?"

"You don't have any idea of how sexy you look right th
minute." He rose from the bed and paced across the har
wood floor. "Your tanned legs stretched out on that ye
low bedspread, your breasts loose, your skin smelling lik
morning dew, your hair tousled. And your eyes. Lad
your dark eyes are black magic, making promises I car
believe you'll keep. And you aren't even aware you'
doing it."

Her eyes had widened as he spoke, and Nick force
himself to look away. He had to move. A hundred-ya
dash would have been a relief. He settled for wide strid
across the bedroom floor.

"Now I've gone and upset you," he muttered. "Dam
mit, Erica, I didn't mean to act like a jerk. I wanted to help
I didn't mean to come over here and drool. I know th
presentation tonight is important to you. I know that. An

n a grown man, pushing forty. I ought to be able to con-
ol myself."

"Nick—"

"It's okay. I've got it out of my system. Everything's un-
er control."

"Nick—"

"How about this? If I start getting out of hand, you just
ll me to stop. Right? You just tell me."

"Nick!"

He stopped pacing and stared at her. "Yes, Erica?"

"I dare you to kiss me."

Without a second thought he was beside her on the bed.
is arms slipped behind her back. "Double-dare."

Mesmerized with anticipation, she gazed into his gold-
ecked eyes. Slowly he lowered his mouth toward hers.
here was still ample time for her to protest. As prom-
ed, he was not forcing himself upon her. If she could push
e words from her throat, she could easily tell him to stop.

Her back, where it rested against the soft pillows and
rimrose coverlet, went rigid. Her fingers curled into tight
sts. What had she been thinking of when she had dared
m? This was insanity. She must tell him to stop.

Yet when his lips touched hers, it was as if he'd struck a
atch to a short fuse. All semblance of her resolve van-
hed in a wisp of smoke, and she knew it was only a mat-
r of moments until the explosion.

His first kiss was light, a gentle teasing with his tongue.
hen her lips parted.

The time for restraint ended. His second kiss was in-
nse. Her mouth, her flesh, her tongue longed to become
part of him.

Her muscles tensed, she tightened her arms around his
ack, seizing him, absorbing his strength. Though her
ovements felt driven and frenzied, their passion was ex-

quisitely choreographed. Not at all clumsy or groping. A
his tongue filled her mouth, her swollen breast fitted pre
cisely into his palm. It was as if their flesh were meant t
join. Her fingers splayed across the hard muscles of h
back and slid along his torso to his tapered waist.

He whispered, tickling her ear with the low, husky v
brations of his voice. "That was a double-dare, wasn't it?

She nodded.

"Are you ready to leap?" he asked.

She blinked up at him. Never before had a man seeme
so utterly perfect to her. His jaw was strong and deter
mined. His eyes glowed enticingly. He was everythin
she'd ever wanted in a man. Strong, self-assured and ur
deniably virile.

"Yes, Nick. I'm ready."

She knew that he offered this pause as an invitation t
her protest. If she didn't truly wish to pursue their lov
making, she could speak now. Or forever hold her peac

"I want you, Nick."

A smile played across his lips. "Thank God. I wasn't su
if I could stop."

She lifted her arms above her head, and he eased th
tank top from her body, revealing her naked flesh inch b
inch until he had stripped away the simple garment.

"Beautiful," he murmured. "Beautiful Erica."

He trailed kisses down her slender throat to her breast
where the dark, round nipples had hardened to ultrasen
sitivity. When his lips first touched her there, she recoile
with a gasp.

"Erica?" He looked up at her face. "Did I hurt you?"

"Don't stop." In a way he had hurt her. She wanted hi
so much that every part of her body was aching with d
sire, and the only relief was more of him.

A nearly unbearable tension built within her when his mouth returned to her breasts. His tongue circled each peak until they throbbed in sweet agony. She lay back on the pillow and moaned with pleasure. "Oh, God, Nick. I want to see you. Your body."

She glided into a sitting position, gently easing him away from her. Her fingers worked at the buttons on his shirt until it gaped, and she pushed away the light cotton material to reveal the thick, curling hair on his tanned chest. She stared, entranced by the incredible variance between them, the wonderful differences between male and female. He was hard, broad and solid. Her body was more delicate, slender. They were such dissimilar beings, and yet she desired everything that he was.

Her excitement was so tremendous that her usually capable hands became clumsy tools, unable to manage the catch on his belt, to unzip his trousers. She fell back on the bed. "You're going to have to help me with this."

"My pleasure."

"And mine."

As he peeled off his clothing she watched, fascinated with his body, his flesh. It seemed as though she had never before seen a naked man. It felt like the first time, and surely this was the first time she had been so intimately aroused, so ready.

He took a small package from his wallet and in an instant had slipped a flesh-colored sheath over his manhood.

"God, that was sexy," she whispered.

"And safe."

"And thoughtful."

He unhooked the buttons of her Levi's and in a single movement removed her panties and cutoff shorts. She lay naked beneath his gaze.

Very gentle and deliberately he positioned himself at the foot of the bed. He kissed the arch of her foot, and she felt shock waves spiraling from her toes to the top of her head. With her other leg she rubbed against him. Then he caught that foot and ran his finger along the soft instep.

He spread her legs and kissed the inside of each knee. He trailed his lips upward along her inner leg to the juncture of her thighs. At the first flicking motion of his tongue she cried out. She reached back; her fingers clutched the railing of her headboard and she held on for dear life, awash in the most excruciating pleasure she'd ever experienced. Beyond imagination. Beyond description.

He tantalized her most secret flesh with his tongue, licking and circling. So consuming was the power of her emotions that she lay perfectly still while every fiber of her body screamed for release. Her fingers tightened on the headboard. Her breath was coming in gasps. Within her a series of explosions began, rippling through every cell of her being. She was utterly alive, living totally in this exquisite moment.

Gracefully he covered her with his body. The hair on his chest tickled her breasts. His torso pressed into her slender waist. Her legs remained splayed and trembling against his hardness.

When he kissed her mouth, deeply and thoroughly, her stillness shattered in a burst of ecstatic motion. She clutched his back. Her fingers clawed. Her pelvis ground against him, aching and throbbing with her need for him.

He entered her, and Erica gasped. Her eyelids flew open as she looked up at him. Into his face. His golden eyes. Her breath came in shallow pants as she felt him move within her.

Their gazes remained locked as their bodies joined. His hardness thrust within her, and she arched greedily against him. He pulled back and thrust again. And again.

Her tongue crept out to moisten her lips as she stared into his eyes, reading a reflection of her own excitement. Breathing hard, he bored into her with his eyes.

Supporting his weight on his elbows, he thrust and she moved against him, encouraging his rhythm. Then, when she felt she could stand it no longer, he mirrored her passion with sweet, fulfilling climax. For a moment they went still, poised for the final satisfaction. An abundant peacefulness washed over them in gentle, concentric waves.

In the aftermath they held each other and trembled together, swept away by the force of their joining, their incredible lovemaking.

He kissed her lightly and eased his weight from her body, taking a position beside her on the bed.

"Wow," he said softly.

"Double wow," she whispered.

"I hope that doesn't mean that I go first, because I don't think I can do this again. Not for a few minutes, anyway."

She snuggled against him. From the first stirrings of her attraction toward him, she'd known that their lovemaking would be spectacular, but never in her wildest fantasies had she expected anything like this.

"How are you feeling?" he asked.

"Wonderful." She dropped a little kiss on his shoulder.

"Not nervous?"

"Why should I be nervous?" She was floating on pink, fluffy clouds, utterly content with the world.

"About tonight."

"Tonight?" she murmured, then sat bolt upright. "Oh, my God! The presentation. What time is it?"

In unison they turned to the bedside clock.

"We need to leave in twenty minutes," he said.

"Twenty minutes!"

She dove from the bed and charged into the bathroom. A quick glance in the mirror told her that she needed another quick shower. Before she plunged under the hot water, she hesitated, hating to wash away the scent of their lovemaking. Yet it might not create the best first impression to appear at the Adventurers' Club smelling of lust. She scrubbed with almond-scented soap.

Her speech. What was the first line of her speech? What came after "Pleased to be here with you tonight?" Rivulets of water coursed down her tender breasts, and she spoke aloud, "'Uganda, Tanzania, Kenya. The natural rain forest habitats of chimpanzee and gorilla are rapidly disappearing from the earth. Despite any good intention on the part of the native governments, they cannot refuse the financial rewards to be gained by harvesting the timber in these forests. Consequently the unique opportunity to study these primates in their natural setting becomes less and less feasible with every season.'"

Good, she told herself. She remembered. At this point she would show slides of the lush vegetation in the central African rain forests.

She heard knocking at the door. "Erica? Are you all right?"

"No problem, Nick. I'm talking to myself."

Behind the shower curtain she heard the door to the bathroom open. "Talking to yourself?"

"Trying to remember my speech. Now go away."

She heard him chuckling as he left and closed the door behind him. Perhaps the most endearing time in this incredible dusky afternoon had been Nick's surprising sensitivity before they'd made love. He had paced like a caged chimp, fighting his natural urges, truly concerned about doing what was best for her.

She left the shower, dried herself and wrapped herself in a towel to scamper into the bedroom. Nick was nowhere in sight, and she shut the bedroom door, dressing quickly. Then it was back to the bathroom to apply a dash of makeup. Mascara, blush and lipstick. Though she would have preferred a more complete face shaping, she knew better than to experiment. Besides, whenever she tried a more complete makeup, she felt like a clown. It was better to be herself.

Erica stared at her reflection in the mirror. She was glowing. She tried to pull her mouth into a scowl and laughed at the silly-looking result. She hoped the Adventurers' Club wouldn't hold this adventure against her.

After adding small gold earrings and a necklace, she fled to the living room, where Nick sat reading over her notes. "This is really good," he said. "And you look terrific."

"But do I look responsible and efficient?"

"If you told me you were capable of balancing the national debt, I'd believe you."

"I hope the Adventurers' Club members feel the same way."

He came to her, placed his hands firmly on her shoulders and peered into her eyes. "You're going to do well, Erica. I know you are."

"I wish I were so sure."

"Let's get 'em, tiger."

He was the tiger, she thought. A dynamic predator. He must have been unstoppable on Wall Street. A bear or a bull? She could never remember which was which but easily imagined Nick harnessing the strength of either beast. It was difficult to believe that he was, as he said, semiretired.

His brand of strength couldn't be set aside on a shelf. It was too much a part of him. Laid-back and settled down? Not hardly!

His gold-flecked eyes gleamed with energy. Beneath his gaze, she could feel his strength. When he touched her, it radiated from his fingertips through her body as if their lovemaking had imparted his power and invincibility to her.

"Before we leave, Nick, I want to tell you that I don't regret what happened between us this afternoon. I didn't expect it, but the time must have been right."

"Must've been." He ran his finger down her cheek. "I guess you can't plan these things."

"Humans try."

"And we're only human," he said.

5

DURING THE DRIVE to the Adventurers' Club, Nick surprised her twice. The first shock was his car—an elegant, cream-colored Mercedes sedan. Two days before, when he'd taken her home from the amusement park with Sheena in tow, they'd ridden in a rattletrap Jeep Wagoneer. "Pretty classy car for an organ-grinder," she said.

"Those years in Manhattan were very good to me."

The second surprise crept up on her.

While he teased and joked and kept her talking, Erica realized that, despite his easygoing manner, Nick was working hard to defuse her nervousness. He was careful not to be condescending or to hold her hand patronizingly. Nonetheless his caring was quite evident.

She wouldn't have predicted this sort of behavior from him, especially not after they'd made love. From such a dominant male, she'd half expected him to act like a chimp—hooting and swaggering and demanding they do it again immediately. Instead he was behaving like a mature, sensitive man. And she liked him for it. Liked him very much.

Perhaps she was beginning to like him too much. A fantastic affair wouldn't disturb her career goals, but she didn't dare consider the implications of a committed relationship. How could she? Her dream of studying in Africa would never be in sync with Nick's semiretirement.

Before Erica could work herself into a dither, she derailed her thoughts of the distant future. There were other, more immediate concerns. Her presentation, for one.

"Nick, do you think I should conclude with 'I appreciate your consideration,' or a more direct approach, more demanding?"

"Taking them hostage might be effective. Of course, this bunch would probably enjoy it. There's one old guy, Dr. Arthur Windom, who actually was a hostage once. Ironic, though. Windom traveled all over the Middle East during the height of terrorist activity, but he was taken hostage in a little town in Nebraska during a bank robbery."

He continued with amusing anecdotes until they reached their destination. The Adventurers' Club met on the third floor of a charmingly renovated older building, north of downtown Denver in an area populated with artists' lofts and unique shops. It was known as LoDo—lower downtown.

In the fading light of early evening Erica climbed from the car and gazed toward the west, where a magenta-and-gold sunset emblazoned the long, trailing clouds above the Rocky Mountains. "Red sky at night," she said, "a sailor's delight."

"A good omen," he agreed. "Not that you need luck. Erica, you are prepared, qualified and ready."

"Thank you." She smiled up at him gratefully. "For everything."

She took his arm, and they entered the building where the Adventurers' Club met to discuss and to dine. It didn't take more than a cursory look for Erica to realize that Nick was right: The Adventurers were a very eclectic group. One handsome middle-aged man wore a tuxedo and comported himself like a real-life James Bond. Several members wore Olympic blazers, T-shirts and sweat clothes. A tall woman, clad in walking shorts and combat boots, identified herself as a militant Greenpeace volunteer.

After several introductions to an archaeologist, a mountain climber and a former astronaut, Nick directed her to the head table, where he protectively took a seat at her right. On her left was Dr. Arthur Windom, a peppery little man who was the club chairman. From Dr. Windom's abrupt spurts of conversation, Erica gathered that he had recently returned from South Africa and that his business there had something to do with diamond mines.

"Poachers," he snapped. "Damn nuisances."

"A bit more than that," Erica corrected gently. "The poachers have done horrifying damage to the indigenous animal population in Africa."

"That's so," he barked.

"Of course, poachers are only one piece of the overall problem. As long as there's a demand for young chimps for research and entertainment, poaching continues to be profitable. Even though taking a baby chimp means killing the mother. Even though only one out of eight of these stolen babies survives."

"You don't approve of mercenary activity?"

Erica felt Nick's hand at her elbow as he commented, "Dr. Windom has been involved worldwide in mercenary actions."

She turned to study the small but rugged man seated to her left. Dr. Windom was the acknowledged leader of this group. Though he was compact, she noted a confidence in the set of his shoulders, his stubborn chin, the ferocious glint in his eyes. Her instincts warned her to back off, to tread lightly with him. But she couldn't. Though she might be blowing her presentation before she'd shown a single slide, Erica couldn't pretend complaisance on this issue.

"Dr. Windom, I am aware that the African nations desperately need an influx of cash. However, because of the profit seeking of poachers and the lumber companies that are destroying the rain forests, chimps are now on the endangered species list. A female chimpanzee reproduces only once every three to five years, and the killing of these adult females is a devastating waste. Given that context, I must say that I do not approve of mercenaries—people who work for profit without concern for the consequences."

Windom glared at her. "A principled sort, aren't you?"

"More practical than principled. Disregard for nature will, I feel, ultimately harm the human population of the world."

Windom's thin lips split in a grin. "I appreciate that, Ms Swanson. And Nickie here paints an unfair picture of me. My so-called mercenary adventures have always been for the betterment of man's condition."

"Like working with the authorities who capture and prosecute the poachers?"

"Haven't done that one yet, but I might. Since I'm fortunate enough to be wealthy, I select my causes based on their worthiness. Like you."

"Not exactly," she said. "I need money."

"Are you prepared to speak?"

"Yes, I am."

Windom marched to the podium and called for attention. While he introduced old business and new, Erica watched the reactions of the audience. During his terse remarks, they were alternately fussy, contentious, approving and pouting. They seemed to disagree on everything, and their diversity dismayed her. How could this group come to an agreement on her proposal? Or on anything?

During this meandering business meeting she learned that Nick was, in fact, a bona fide member of the Adventurers' Club. Four years ago he'd participated in a deep-sea living expedition, searching for Atlantis.

"Atlantis?" she murmured sardonically.

"If you're really nice," he whispered back, "I'll show you my sea-soaked pottery shards."

"Your crockery?"

"You're not the only one with impossible dreams."

Nick toyed with his fork, only half paying attention to the proceedings as he remembered the idyllic Atlantis expedition near the Canary Islands. The weather had been perfect, without a single squall to ruffle the endless blue horizon, and the soundless world beneath the sea was a golden memory. Though he didn't rediscover Atlantis, Nick had found an abiding inner peace during that trip. Peace and pottery shards. The expedition had marked a change in him, the first inkling that his life as a Wall Street stockbroker wasn't altogether satisfying.

Tonight he had a similar sense that his life wasn't exactly satisfactory. Something important was lacking, and he knew that only Erica could fill the void. But a relationship with her was another impossible quest, a mythic seeking after that which was beyond his grasp.

She had made it extremely clear that she couldn't be tied down. Yes that was exactly what he wanted. He wanted to bind her to him, to make her an indivisible part of himself, to become a family.

He turned toward Dr. Windom. Erica was sitting one seat closer to the podium, and Nick's focus quickly wandered to a study of her dark curly hair, her tiny gold earring, the arch of her back beneath the blue silk dress. His

glimpse of her profile was tantalizing, and he found himself becoming aroused simply by looking at her. He
couldn't wait to make love to her again. When Windom
announced her presentation, Nick leaned forward and
gave her hand an encouraging squeeze.

She spoke very well. Though informative, her talk was
also entertaining, spiced with wit. At one point she asked
the Adventurers to echo a hooting jungle cry, and the
group didn't need much encouragement. Chimp shrieks
resounded. Though her slides fell short of professional
expertise, they served nicely to illustrate the points she was
making. Her only real stumbling block came in the ques-
tion-and-answer period.

"Ms Swanson," came a voice from the audience. "It
seems that your research at the zoo is coming along very
well. Why do you wish to abandon that project?"

"That research would continue," she said. "I would train
someone else to take my place."

"Another anthropologist?"

"Probably not," she admitted. "The zoo budget pre-
cludes hiring highly trained individuals. And most pri-
matologists would prefer to set up their own methodology
for study."

"You claim that your findings are of value, but you're
willing to dump the project on a nonprofessional?"

"May I point out that Jane Goodall herself didn't have
a university degree when she began her studies on the
Gombe River. Of course, she was under the tutelage of the
renowned archaeologist and paleontologist Louis Leakey."

"Comparing yourself to Leakey?"

Erica grinned. "Leakey was famous worldwide, especially on the vast continent of Africa. I'm famous at the
several acres of the Golden Independent Zoo."

Appreciative chuckles greeted her remark, but Nick could see that the damage had been done. Erica's devotion to research had been called into question.

IN THE CAR after her speech she turned to him. "What do you think? How did it go?"

"Your presentation was outstanding. I really liked the part when you did ape noises."

"But will they fund me?"

"I would. But, then, I'm not impartial. I would also walk a million miles for one of your smiles."

"Seriously, Nick. You know these people."

"I wish I could give you a guarantee. But they're very unpredictable."

She flopped back against the seat. "Damn. I should have dealt with the issue of my zoo research. I really ought to be training someone right now to take over. But I can't ask Amanda to hire another person. I know she's financially strapped."

"Shall we continue this discussion at my place or yours?"

"It's after eleven o'clock, Nick."

"I might not be a professional observer, but I can tell time." He faked an exaggerated double take. "Or are you trying to tell me that you have a headache?"

For the past three days he had been constantly in her thoughts. And their lovemaking in the afternoon had been superlative. Now she was plagued by reluctance—a combination of after-speaking letdown and exhaustion from her hectic preparations.

More than that. She had a niggling fear in the back of her mind that she should not get too close to this man. There was an ever present danger of involvement. When he pulled up at a stoplight, she touched his arm. "This is all moving a little too fast for me."

"Then fasten your seat belt and hang on." He captured her hand and raised it to his lips. "I won't hurt you, Erica. You'll be safe with me. I promise."

"I trust you. Lord knows why, but I do trust you."

"Woman's intuition?"

She scoffed. "Instinct."

They rode together in silence through the streets of Denver. Since it was a warm summer Friday night, there was other traffic, but the air-cooled Mercedes felt self-contained, a cocoon that protected them from the rest of the world.

She leaned back on the soft leather seat and wondered. Instinct played a huge part in her emotional state. His maleness undeniably summoned her natural urges. But there was more. Being with Nick felt very, very right. Why else would she have made love after knowing him such a short time? Why else would she trust him so blindly? She had the feeling that she'd boarded a roller coaster that was climbing slowly, inexorably to the pinnacle before the first dive. If she didn't step off, there would be no stopping the wild, plunging ride.

She needed to think of her career, to remember the course she'd set for herself. She blurted out, "Nick, I want to go to Africa. I'm thirty-two years old. I can't wait much longer."

"A biological time clock? I thought most women associated that with childbearing."

"I'm not like most women."

"You can say that again."

He drove down the street to her apartment building and parked in the lot. "May I accompany you upstairs?"

"No," she said immediately. "Because if you do, I'll ask you to come in, then I'll offer you a drink and you'll accept, and we'll end up in bed together."

"Is that so bad?"

"Oh, no, not bad. This afternoon was unbelievably good."

"Then why not, Erica? Don't deny yourself. Don't deny me."

"I need to think about it. I need space."

She didn't want to fall in love with him. There wasn't time in her life for a relationship, for a family. Then she looked at him. The glow from a streetlamp highlighted his cheekbones and the firmness of his jaw. Before she could blink, her goals and dreams reshaped themselves to include his image. Though she warned herself to look away before she caved in to his desire, her instincts kept her gazing. With a burst of willpower she said, "We should say good-night right now."

"If that's what you want."

"It's what I need to do."

He unfastened her seat belt and pulled her toward him. Despite her resolve, she came willingly, closer and closer. An impending sense of calamity rose within her, but when their lips met, she forgot all else. The seductive promise of his embrace churned her sensory memory as she tasted his seductive promise of his embrace churned her sensory memory as she tasted his honeyed lips. When his hand cupped her breast, drawing teasing circles on the blue silk bodice that lightly covered her taut nipple, she felt the stirrings of another powerful explosion.

"Erica," he whispered, "we're both too old to be making out in the car."

From deep within came her answer. "I have to go now."

"All right." His lips left her mouth bereft. His hand departed from her breast. "Then good night, Erica."

Her instinct clamored for more, demanded that she take him to her apartment, to her bed. Yet her voice was calm. "Will I see you in the morning? When Michael comes to the zoo?"

"Maybe." His hands gripped the steering wheel. "Saturday's a busy day at the park."

"You're not angry, are you?"

"I suppose not." He stared through the windshield, avoiding her gaze. "I don't have a right to be angry, do I?"

She touched his shoulder. "I'm pleased about tonight. Even if the Adventurers' Club doesn't give me a grant, it was good practice to present my material."

"Good night, Erica." His voice was husky. "Sleep well."

She felt him watching her as she left the Mercedes, opened the lobby door with her key and hurried inside. After she'd dashed up the stairs and flicked on the light in her apartment, she ran to her bedroom window. The Mercedes was gone.

"Good night, Nick."

6

BY TWO O'CLOCK the following afternoon Erica had decided that Nick's son, Michael, was something of a pest. His attitude—from the moment he arrived at the zoo in the morning—personified a teenager's idea of "cool," with no excitement allowed. Behind his sunglasses his features remained frozen. He walked in a slouch. Any attempt at conversation brought a monosyllabic reply.

Because of her experience with her brothers and sisters, Erica had recognized the pose and had treated it by giving Michael a vast number of tasks: picking up litter, collecting and dumping the trash containers, swabbing up after the buffalo and feeding the camels.

He performed without complaining but asked no questions and made no comments. Though she guessed Michael was maintaining his distance partly because he was unsure about the effect of her relationship with his father, the teenager's attitude was still annoying. The only time he'd smiled was when Sheena crawled into his arms, stared into his eyes and offered him a banana.

At midafternoon Michael and Sheena, wearing her leash and harness, walked hand in hand behind Erica toward Primate Island. Erica climbed over the fence. "Okay, Michael, it's time for me to take Sheena to the island, where I hope she'll interact with the other chimps."

"I'll carry her across."

"I'm sorry, but I can't allow that."

"Great," he muttered. "You get to do all the fun stuff, and I get to clean up after the buffalo."

"Listen here, young man, there's a great deal to be learned by observing, even from watching the stinky old buffalo. And if you aren't interested, if you don't love being around animals, you might as well go home right now."

"My dad wouldn't like it if you sent me home."

"I didn't invite you here to impress your father."

"Oh, yeah? Then how come?"

"Because of you, Michael." She struggled to contain her annoyance with him. "Maybe I was wrong, but I thought I saw something in you."

"Like what?"

"A certain attitude. A caring. Curiosity mixed with patience. I thought you'd work well with the animals."

"Then how come I can't take Sheena to the island?"

"Because you have a lot to learn. Also because these chimps can't be trusted. Lenny, the adult male, is only four feet tall, but he's three times stronger than you or me. New caretakers have to be introduced slowly and with consistency. If you want to work with them, you have to make a serious commitment."

"Like what kind of commitment?"

"You'd have to spend a week taking them their food, each time wading a step closer to the island. Then another week of just sitting on the very edge of the island. Then, one step at a time, integrating yourself into their group."

"Why don't they like people?"

"It's not a matter of like or dislike. Male chimps are naturally territorial. Lenny might see your presence as a threat to his dominance and charge at you. Or Jenny, the adult female, might be frightened, thinking you were trying to harm her baby. Then she would attack. Only Amanda and I have ever gone onto the island."

Michael fidgeted, shifting from one foot to the other. "I'll do it."

"Pardon me?"

"I'll come back every day and let them get used to me."

"That means every day, Michael. Every single day."

He rewarded her with a genuine smile. "I'll try."

"Okay, we'll try. Now you wait here on the shore while I take Sheena. Cross over to this side of the fence and squat."

He got into position. "Like this?"

"Fine. Now I know this might be difficult, Michael, but try to look pleasant and nonthreatening. And take off those sunglasses."

"Jeez, are you this bossy with my dad?"

She raised her eyebrows as a memory of the previous night and her refusal to invite Nick into her apartment flitted across her mind. "It's not even remotely the same thing, Michael. Your father isn't working with me. You are. Or at least you've said that you want to. And in this situation, I am the boss."

"Okay, Erica."

"Now I might be over on the island for two minutes. But if things go well, it might be a long time. I want you to stay here and observe."

With Sheena on her shoulders Erica headed toward the most shallow part of the moat. It was twelve feet across to the island and two feet deep. Because the stream had been dammed and diverted, the current was negligible.

In an old pair of sneakers, used expressly for this purpose, Erica waded into the delightfully cold water. On these hot July days she loved the chilly moment when the crystal-clear stream flowed against her bare legs.

She glanced over her shoulder at Michael, who gave her a thumbs-up sign and a patently friendly grin.

Apparently they were now buddies. Erica shrugged. Teenagers truly were bizarre creatures, she decided. Michael had been hostile all morning. Now they were pals, and she wasn't sure what had made the difference. His commitment? Chagrined, she realized that his promise to return daily almost meant that she was committed to spending time with him. Every day. No matter what happened with his father.

As usual, a good-size crowd had gathered on the bank to watch this procedure. Also, as usual, Sheena began to shriek as soon as she caught sight of little Java, who was bouncing up and down with excitement.

On the island Erica plucked Sheena from her shoulders and crouched beside a clump of grass. The little female chimp refused to leave her keeper's side, hiding behind Erica and hooting at Java.

Today, however, there was a slight behavioral difference. Java refused to be put off by Sheena's cries. He knuckle-walked toward her and struck out one long finger to touch her arm. Sheena was hysterical. She grabbed a handful of grass and flung it.

Java plucked the grass from his chest and gave her a silly, loose-lipped smile.

Then the baby appeared. Sheena ran toward the tiny chimp and knocked him down. Immediately Jenny, the mother, roared from the bushes and swatted viciously at Sheena.

Erica gathered Sheena in her arms and quickly went back into the stream where the other chimps would not follow. Sheena was no match for an enraged adult female.

Back onshore she handed Sheena over to Michael.

"Is it always like that?" he questioned excitedly.

"No, thank goodness."

The other people who'd been watching came to the fence and were reaching toward Sheena, who cheerfully waved at them. Now that she was back among human beings, the little chimp's equilibrium was quickly restored.

Erica slipped the harness and leash on Sheena before she allowed the animal to interact with the sightseers. "Any questions?"

There were several, and Erica noticed that Michael was listening carefully.

They returned to the chimp's indoor enclosure, a large concrete building with high south-facing windows covered by heavy iron mesh. Erica asked, "Did you learn anything from that?"

"I think, you know, Java is kind of lonesome." He turned to Sheena. "How come you don't like him?"

Sheena scratched her head.

"Maybe he's not her type," Michael said.

"Maybe not." Erica sat at a small desk beneath the windows. "I need to make some notes in my journal, Michael. Why don't you take Sheena into the caged enclosure and let her run around? You'll need to get used to her if you're going to help me."

He took Sheena by the hand but spoke to her keeper. "I think you were right, Erica. I think I'm going to like working with the chimps."

She nodded and concentrated on her journal. In longhand she wrote several paragraphs about the encounter on the island, finally adding a note: "I am considering the possibility of a new caretaker for the chimps. His name is Michael, and he's sixteen years old. Sheena approved of him at first sight, which is similar to the way she reacted to his father."

Slowly Erica closed the journal. What about Michael's father? Why hadn't Nick called her today? He must be angry about last night. His male ego must have been insulted when she didn't readily invite him into her bed. And if that was the way he wanted to play, she was glad to know it. If he intended to sulk every time she didn't do exactly as he wanted, she would let him go. Who needed that additional frustration? Certainly not Erica. She didn't want it. It was better to let him go, cut him loose. She snapped her fingers. Like that.

Yet she sighed when she recalled their lovemaking the previous afternoon. His expert sexuality. That pleasure seemed so far away, almost as if it had never occurred. But it had happened, and she would never forget it.

"Hey, Erica," Michael shouted from behind the wire mesh-enclosed area. "You want to come to dinner tonight? I'm cooking."

She hesitated. Though she hated to consider the possibility, Nick might not want her showing up on his doorstep. He might have other plans. He might not want to see her. "Thank you, Michael. But I really ought to spend this evening with Sheena. It's very possible that her extreme reaction to the other chimps today was because I deviated from her regular schedule yesterday and the day before."

"Sheena can come, too," he said. "She can be my date."

"All right." If Nick didn't want to see her again, it was best that she find out right away. There was no sense in mooning around after a man who was uninterested. "Seven o'clock?"

The remainder of the day passed very slowly, and still Nick didn't phone or send bananas or appear. After Erica had returned home to her apartment with Sheena, she reconsidered Michael's dinner invitation. Obviously Nick was avoiding her. On the other hand, they hadn't made a definite appointment, and he'd warned her that Saturday at Barron's Amusement Park was busy.

"For pity's sake," she said to Sheena. "I'm not Cinderella going to the ball. There's no need to get all hot and bothered about this. It's only dinner."

Sheena hooted and hopped on one foot.

"I'm a mature adult. I can handle it."

"If all she wanted from Nick was a pleasurable physical affair, there was no need to play games, to second-guess him or worry if he didn't telephone. When she saw him, they would simply have to talk over their problems and come to the proper solutions.

Yet when she and her chimp companion stood on the doorstep to the three-story brick house on the residential street opposite the roller coaster at Barron's, Erica's palms began to sweat. Her stomach roiled as she punched the doorbell and told herself that it would be childish to hide behind one of the sculpted shrubs that decorated the thick, healthy lawn.

Michael answered the door wearing a chef's apron that said Nuke Burgers. "I hope you like your food well-done."

He escorted them through the flagstone foyer, where four date palms squatted in huge ceramic tubs. From what she could see, the house was filled with plants. Some exotic, some mundane, but all flourishing. "It's like a jungle in here."

"Yeah, there are four greenhouses behind Barron's, and Dad brings the sick plants home to nurse them."

"These don't look sick."

Sheena hooted her agreement, making a concerted effort to clutch a delicate, blooming orange tree.

"After they're here for a while, he gets attached to them, talks to them all the time and plays his boring music for them. It's real weird." He led her to the rear patio, where a barbecue grill flamed. "Dad says every guy should know how to cook for himself. So we're taking turns every other night."

Erica regarded the blackened hamburger patties on the grill. "Your father is a brave man."

Sheena gave a hooting noise, tugged at her leash and pointed toward a large peach tree beside a robust vegetable garden full of zucchini and tomatoes. The flower beds bordering the lawn offered an incredible blooming array. Altogether it was a very tempting Eden for a chimp. "It might be best, Michael, if we took Sheena indoors."

"The basement," he said, lifting the burgers onto a plate with a spatula. "I figured we could eat down there."

As they followed Michael through the kitchen and down the stairs, Erica was dying to ask if Nick was home. She couldn't help peering around corners and glancing over her shoulder. Her body was on sensory alert. She thought she heard the patter of a rushing shower, the buzz of an electric razor. Amid the profusion of fragrant plants and flowers, she imagined the scent of his after-shave. The sense of his nearness was tantalizing, and her heart rate accelerated with each passing moment.

"Here we go," Michael said, escorting them into a spacious room and closing the door. Down here there were only a few ferns hung by the high windows. Furniture was minimal, but the walls were brightened with an array of posters. The room looked like the sort of space designed for a teenage party. Or a gathering of chimps.

"This is perfect," Erica said.

"Yeah, I moved everything that could be broken."

He had also arranged paper plates and plastic ware on a Ping-Pong table, and Erica noted that there were five place settings. That meant Nick was expected for dinner

She released Sheena from her leash. Immediately the little beast explored the room, finding the Ping-Pong paddles and banging them together over her head. "I'm afraid," Erica said, "that Sheena isn't the most polite dinner guest."

"Hey, she's a lot more exciting than people. Does she like music?"

"Yes, but I try not to play it too loudly around her. Remember, Michael, the idea is for Sheena to learn how to be a chimp, not to be more like us."

"Right. I'll get the fruit salad and be right back."

Michael bustled from the room, carefully closing the door behind him so Sheena couldn't escape.

"Very thoughtful," Erica murmured. "Sheena, I think Michael is going to be terrific at zoo work."

Sheena stared up at the hanging plants. Fortunately they were beyond her grasp, even when she bounded toward them.

Still keeping a watchful eye on the little ape, Erica perched on the bench beside the Ping-Pong table. Almost immediately she was back on her feet, too edgy to sit still. Was Nick going to be here? Of course he'd be here; it was his house and his charred burgers. What would she say to him? The word "yes" popped into her mind. No matter what he said or did, she would say "yes." Great, she chastised herself, that was a terrific way to maintain control of their relationship.

"No," she said, forcing the word through her lips, and Sheena swung around to stare at her. In spite of her tension, Erica laughed. "I'm as bad as you are with Java."

Sheena turned a somersault and followed as Erica prowled around the room. The habitat, she thought, Nick's natural habitat. What did it say about him? The only conclusive statement must be that he loved plants and had a green thumb.

Two walls of the basement room were papered with colorful posters of rock bands and fast cars, but those were probably Michael's. On the wall above a battered old desk hung a grouping of photographs. A formal eight-by-ten portrait of Michael as a pudgy blond toddler, Nick in a tailored navy suit and a woman caught her eye. The woman was lovely. A pale, dainty blonde with doelike brown eyes. She must be Nick's ex-wife.

With a twinge of regret Erica stared at the smiling faces in the photograph. She would never have that life, never have a beaming family to sit beside her and say cheese for a photographer's lens. Her course was different. She was thirty-two and fully intended to spend the next several years in the African jungles, pursuing her research. Alone.

In another photograph Nick, wearing a baggy swimsuit and sporting a healthy tan, stood on the deck of a boat. His hair was lightened by the sun and disheveled by the wind. His chin was dark with several days' growth of beard. This must be a photo from his Atlantis expedition.

Erica took it off the wall for closer study. This was yet another side of Nick Barron, a side that greatly appealed to her. Here he looked like an adventurer, a modern-day pirate. She could imagine this man on safari with her, whacking through the rain forests with a machete.

"No." She replaced the picture on the wall. That was too much to hope for.

When the basement door opened, Erica whipped around. Though she was mature and logical and prepared to see him, the sight of Nick disconcerted her. He stepped through the doorway, carrying a massive bowl of fruit salad. His golden eyes were bright and alive. "Good evening, Erica."

Forty thousand shades of emotions whirled within her like a fragmented rainbow: excitement, confusion, irritation, happiness. But all she could say was "Hello, Nick."

He kicked the door closed and set the bowl on the Ping-Pong table. "It was a beautiful day today, wasn't it?"

The word "yes" was on the tip of her tongue. "Not really. It was awfully hot."

"Are you tired after last night?"

Yes. "Not at all. I slept well."

"I missed you today," he said.

"I was at the zoo. All day."

"Michael told me." His lips curved in a devastatingly handsome smile. "I appreciate what you're doing with him."

"As I told Michael, I'm not working with him to please you." The words sounded more harsh than she'd intended. "Michael seems to have a gift for zoo work. I can't ignore that."

"Of course not."

They stood two feet apart, each drinking in the other's presence. He took a step toward her, bridging the scant distance between them. His hand rose to caress her cheek.

The pleasure of his gentle touch was so reassuring that she sighed, almost purred like a contented pussycat. She placed her fingers lightly upon his chest and leaned toward him, yearning for his embrace.

Then Sheena was beside them. She flung her long arms clumsily around Nick's waist and bared her strong white teeth, making a "hee-hee-hee" sound.

"Yes, Sheena. Hello." Nick scratched the course black hair on her head. "Did I ignore you?"

She continued her "hee-hee" and pulled him to the door, sensing that Michael would enter. When he did, Sheena detached herself from Nick to fawn around his son's knees.

Nick shrugged. "Fickle, isn't she? I guess what they say is true."

"Oh? And what do they say?"

"'Heaven has no rage like love to hatred turned, nor hell a fury like a chimp scorned.'"

Love to hatred turned, Erica mentally repeated. Not lust, but love. She liked the sound of the word from his lips. Love. No, not love. She shouldn't be thinking of love. Why couldn't she get this straightened out in her head?

"Sorry I didn't get over to the zoo today," he said. "We were short on employees, and I spent the entire day running the carousel."

"No problem," she lied. "I wasn't really expecting you."

While Michael and Sheena raced upstairs to fetch the buns and catsup, Nick regarded her sardonically. "Weren't you just a little disappointed when I didn't show up?"

Yes, she silently answered, *I was bereft.* "No," she said. "Not in the least."

"I was. Disappointed and lonely. I couldn't get you out of my head. And I want to see you tonight. At your apartment."

The word she'd been suppressing leaped from her throat. "Yes. Yes, Nick. Later tonight. I'd like that."

Their dinner of burned burgers and runny fruit salad tasted like ambrosia to her.

7

THOUGH NICK ARRIVED after Sheena had been safely locked into her own bedroom, Erica felt foolishly guilty—as if she shouldn't be entertaining a man while the chimp was in the apartment. She shushed him at the door. "I'm not sure if Sheena is asleep."

"Chimps aren't nocturnal, are they?"

"No, Sheena enjoys a good night's sleep much as a human being would, but I don't often have guests after her bedtime. I'm not sure if she'll wake up."

"Not in front of the chimps or the children?" He chuckled. "I understand. All through dinner I had to fight the urge to ravish your gorgeous body because Michael was watching."

She collapsed into a chimp-battered chair and glanced around her living room. Long ago she'd given up drapes because the dangling material was too tempting for Sheena. Nor did she dare hang breakable, glass-covered pictures on the walls. Her only attempt at decor was a plastic mobile suspended from the ceiling beyond Sheena's reach. As a rule, her home's plain interior didn't bother her. But tonight she wished for something more romantic, with soft colors and candlelight. Her apartment seemed a harsh environment to discuss a relationship. "Was there ever a more complicated affair?"

"Doubtful." He sat opposite her. "I've got a confused teenage son, and you've got an equally confused chimp."

"At least that's almost something in common."

"Are we that different?" he asked.

"You've got to be joking! For a start, you like quiet guitar solos, and I'm a fan of rock 'n' roll. You're semiretired. I'm still waiting for my life to happen. You like carbonated sodas. I drink water."

"I like being settled down. You want to go to Africa."

"To-may-to," she said, testing.

"To-mah-to."

"I want a relationship," he said. "You want an affair."

The teasing was gone from his manner, and his golden eyes regarded her seriously. "That's the big one, isn't it? None of the rest really matters when we throw it up against that difference."

"But it's part of the same problem, Nick. Don't you see? If I didn't want to go to Africa, there would be nothing standing in the way of a relationship."

"No, I don't see," he said bluntly. "There's no such thing as a perfect match between a man and a woman. And, to be frank, the surprises are half the fun. Wouldn't it be boring if we were compatible in every way?"

"Yes," she said. "It would."

With her ex-husband she'd already experienced a precise match. Not only did his archaeological career coincide with her animal studies, but also their mental processes were almost a mirror reflection of each other. He seemed to know what she was thinking before she said it. Within two months of their marriage they'd almost stopped talking altogether. Then they'd divorced, and she'd found the glass jackal to add to her collection. Symbolically the joke had been on her. The perfect match didn't exist, except perhaps in a textbook.

At least, she thought, she wasn't making the same mistake twice. She and Nick were different. Excitingly different. How should she symbolize her moments with him?

Perhaps a tiger for their passion. Or a cowering mouse to stand for her fear of commitment. Maybe, she feared, a broken heart.

"What was it like," she asked, "with your ex-wife?"

He raised his eyebrows. "Where did that thought come from?"

"I saw a family photo in the basement room. She's a beautiful woman."

"Very pretty," he agreed. "Tall and slim and blond. She had her hair trimmed just so. And she never left the house without makeup."

"Feminine?"

"Yes. Catherine was very dainty."

Erica scrunched down in her chair, silently acknowledging her hopeless inadequacy in that department. Though her sisters had tried to teach her the wiles of femininity, she'd never understood the secrets of kohl-lined eyes and smooth makeup foundation. Her hair was styled for simplicity of care, not glamour. She hated wearing high heels and panty hose. "Not like me."

"You're feminine," he said with an ardor that shocked her. "One of the most female creatures I know."

"How can you say that? Look at this room."

"Femininity isn't all that froufrou. It's something inside. Being comfortable with yourself as a woman. When I look around this room, I see a woman who is caring. A woman who believes enough in herself that she doesn't worry about what the neighbors might think. You know who you are."

Erica was still unconvinced. "Unfortunately that won't show up in a photograph."

"But it's true. You are womanly. And I know because the woman in you summons up the man in me." He leaned back in the chair and folded his arms across his chest.

"Whenever I'm around you, I've got to hold myself back. I want to touch you. All the time. I want to feel your feminine body in my arms. To kiss your soft, female lips."

He had to look away from her. Tilting his head back, he stared up at the ceiling. How could she not know? Every time he got near her, his self-control went haywire. Not feminine? Even while he looked up at the plain light fixture he could imagine the womanly curve of her hips and the sweet perfection of her breasts.

Of course she was different from his ex-wife. Catherine had been preoccupied with appearance, so intent on how things looked that she ignored how they felt. She was a good woman, a good mother for Michael. But he didn't miss her company.

He lowered his gaze to study Erica. Physically, she and his ex-wife were very different. While Catherine had been blond and svelte, Erica's tanned body exuded healthy energy. Catherine was given to clever manipulations. Erica was direct. Her self-sufficiency excited him. She wouldn't hesitate to charge forth and grab what she wanted. To fight for it. More than anything in the world, he wanted her on his side, by his side. He wanted an alliance, a relationship.

"Let me sum it up," he said. "Catherine and I will always be connected by our love for Michael, but the relationship we shared is gone. In fact, I think she's going to remarry at the end of the year, but that has very little to do with me. I don't think it does much good to talk about past relationships."

"Oh, but it does." Erica pounced on his words. "Learning from the past is an important feature of the human mind."

Gratefully she resorted to a mind set she could understand, arranging their behavior in a clinical pattern of observation. "There are three major behavioral differences between human beings and chimps. Human beings instinctively engage in spoken communication. Human beings can plan for the distant future, and remember the distant past and learn from it."

"Uh-huh." He nodded. "So?"

Erica was growing excited. Finally things were beginning to fall into place. "So if I can learn what went wrong with your first marriage, then I can avoid making the same—" Abruptly she fell silent.

"Go on," he urged.

"No. I'm getting ahead of myself." Mentioning marriage was about twenty miles ahead of where she wanted to be. She bounced to her feet. "Why is this so damn complicated?"

"Well, if we were a couple of chimps in the rain forest, it might be easier. I'd sling you over my shoulder and drag you off into the woods."

"But we're not chimps."

"Not the last time I checked."

"Can't we just allow things to happen?"

He shook his head. "You know we can't. Last night you were responding to me physically, but something in your head wouldn't allow you to make love."

"I needed space. That's natural. Chimps do that, too."

"If you need space, that's fine. I won't crowd you. If you have to go to Tanzania, that's fine, too. I don't want you to give up your career. But I do want a relationship with you, Erica."

"And what does that mean?" She stalked across the grass mats on the floor until she stood directly in front of him, hands on hips. "To me, a relationship means commitment. And I can't do that. I have goals I want to meet, places I want to go. Nick, I don't want to start building a nest if I can't live in it."

"Somehow I have a hunch that you're not a nesting sort of bird. Not a little robin or a duckie or a goose." He rose to his feet and threaded his arms around her waist. "You're an eagle, Erica. And I want to soar by your side. Free and proud. I won't shoot you down."

He pulled her against his chest, but she maintained her implacable hands-on-hips pose, only tilting her head back to look up at him. Even eagles needed mates. "A relationship, huh?"

"With a capital *R*. It's a connection between us that means I care about you and vice versa."

"But no demands?" she questioned. This didn't seem possible. "No promises?"

"Only that you'll make love to me twenty times a day."

"I don't know." She slipped her arms around him. "Twenty times a day sounds like you're already being unrealistic."

"You don't know that. I might be a phenomenal biological specimen, capable of superhuman mating feats. I'd say it was your duty as a student of higher primates to check out my claim."

"Your brag," she corrected.

"Ah, but you don't know that without field study." He glided his hands down her back to her bottom and pressed her hips against his, creating a tantalizing, teasing friction. "What do you say, lady?"

"All right, Nick. I'll agree to a temporary relationship."

"Definition of your terms, please."

She inhaled, catching the scent of his spicy after-shave. Her tension had been released, and she allowed her body to mold to his. "It means, Nick, that I want to be with you while I can."

He lowered his mouth to hers for a light kiss, sealing their arrangement. "It seems like I ought to give you something."

"I feel the same way. There should be some sort of primitive, symbolic ritual of exchange."

He glanced at the gold Rolex watch on his wrist. It had been very expensive, as dear as his feelings for her. Without hesitation he snapped it off his arm and placed it in her hand.

She shook her head. "This is beautiful, Nick, but I can't wear it. It's too big for me. And much too costly for a symbolic gift."

He dug into his trouser pocket and pulled out his key chain. There were two ornaments attached: a silver B for Barron, and an imitation pearl pocketknife—an inexpensive little thing that was used as a prize in the arcade at the amusement park.

Snapping open the chain, he removed the pocketknife, pulled it open to reveal a not-very-sharp blade, then closed it and held it out in his hand. "This is for you, Erica. May thoughtless words or deeds never sunder our...temporary relationship."

She accepted his gift and glided her arms over his chest and around his neck. Her intention was to give him a formal, symbolic sort of kiss. But when their lips met, her natural yearning for him recommenced with a passion. Her mouth worked hungrily over his, insatiably consuming and being consumed. Her tongue plunged deeply, engaging with his. She was driven to embrace him fervently, to press her body against his.

Abruptly she stopped and held him at arm's length. "I could slow down."

His chest was heaving. "That might be nice."

"We have hours and hours." She sparkled and shimmered with a desire that could last for days. For weeks. Temporary, of course, but she was ready for the duration. Their mating could be such fun—sensual fun. He was a natural tease, and she was beginning to feel equally playful. With deliberate slyness she raked her hands down his chest to the waistband of his trousers and hooked her fingers in his belt loops. "Besides," she breathed. "I must give something to you."

"Yourself, Erica, is all I want. All I need."

"Come with me."

Taking his hand, she led him down the hall to her bedroom, unlocked the door and escorted him inside. She went to the small velvet jewel box on her dresser and found a silver chain, which she threaded through a small hole in the handle of the pocketknife. She held it up to show him. "A lavaliere. Will you help me put it on?"

After he fastened the catch at her nape, he caressed her shoulders and turned her to him. The imitation pearl pocketknife hung from her throat. "On you," he said, "it looks good."

"And now it's your turn," she said. From her jewelry box she took the extra key to her apartment. Her fingers closed around it while she considered. This was a huge step, offering him ready access to her inner sanctum, but her misgivings vanished when she gazed into his gold-flecked eyes.

"This is for you," she said, placing the key in his hand. "It opens the front door to my home. Come into my life whenever you wish. My secrets are open to you."

He held the key reverently, as if it were an object of great price. "Thank you, Erica."

She winked. "If I remember correctly, that's not a real thank-you."

"You're right."

He needed no further encouragement. He pulled her into his arms and joined his mouth with hers for a long, deep kiss. Still joined, he carried her to the bed. But when he placed her on the bed, she was again seized by playfulness and she abruptly yanked his shoulders. Off balance, Nick sprawled indelicately across her body on the bed.

"What was that?" he asked.

"Foreplay?"

"Wonderful. For consummation do you intend to break my neck?"

She ruffled his hair. "I want to play with you."

"Is this one of those chimp things?"

"Actually the other primates are somewhat dull in their procreational activities. I think recreational sexuality is a strictly human trait."

She tugged his shirttail free from his pants, slipped her hands beneath the cotton material and . . . tickled him.

He laughed convulsively. "Don't do that."

"You're ticklish." She was delighted. Immediately she bared her midriff. "I'm not. Go ahead and try."

He tickled and she frowned smugly.

"That's only your stomach," he reminded her. "What about your feet?"

"Not ticklish at all."

He peeled off her shoes and tickled the soles of her feet. Though other sensations immediately pinged through her, she had no urge to giggle. One after the other, he removed her garments, attempting to get a chortling rise from her. Finally she was completely naked.

He tickled lightly down her neck, over her breasts and down her torso to her thighs. She couldn't help wriggling under his touch. But she didn't laugh.

"Aha," he said. "You might not be ticklish, but I think I know how to get a response from you."

He bolted from the room. Swiftly he returned. His own clothing had been stripped away, and he had his hands behind his back. "You're going to be sorry you started this."

The mischief in her eyes mingled with desire. "I sincerely doubt that I will."

He arranged himself beside her, subtly pinning her legs beneath his. "Close your eyes," he said.

She did. "I'm not ticklish, Nick. And there's nothing you can do about it."

"We'll see." He managed to catch both her wrists and held them above her head.

Her eyes flew open. "What are you doing?"

He displayed the object he'd held behind his back: a single translucent ice cube.

"You'd better not, Nick. I mean it."

"So do I."

The ice touched the peak of her breast, and an electric thrill went through her. Her sharp intake of breath ended in a pleasured moan when he lowered his mouth to lick away the chill. With the cube he circled her other breast, again producing a high-voltage reaction.

He touched her lips with the ice, parting them and allowing her trembling gasps to escape. She licked at the cube, and a cold trickle slid down her throat.

He drew a low, shivering icy line from her collarbone, between her breasts to her flat stomach. By the time he reached her soft triangle of hair, Erica was trembling all over. Not with cold but with desire.

"It's melted," he said, releasing her wrists.

"So am I."

She flung her arms around him, and when their naked flesh met, she experienced a complete happiness. She'd done the right thing by making this temporary commitment. No longer did she need to hold back. She was free to adore his masculine body, to fully accept his skillful touch. If this ecstasy represented a temporary relationship, she didn't dare imagine the wonder of a full-scale commitment. The fulfillment would be more than she could bear.

After they made love, she lay still beside him, cheerfully contemplating what came next. The future lay before her like the white unmarked pages of her journal, and it would be up to Erica to write her destiny in bold strokes.

A single doubt shadowed the sunny future. If she won the grant from the Adventurers' Club, it meant that she would leave Nick. She shifted and snuggled against him. When she went to Africa—and she was confident that someday her work and perseverance would prevail—she would travel alone.

It seemed that leaving him to fulfill her lifelong career dream was something of a contradiction. Why should she have to abandon their relationship? To exchange one dream for another?

He moved against her, arousing her with light kisses. She would have to be insane to willingly give up this pleasure. Her fingers closed around the little pocketknife that hung from the chain around her neck.

8

DURING THE THREE WEEKS that followed, the drama of a first tentative commitment gradually developed into a behavioral pattern between Erica and Nick—a pattern that, of course, included Michael and Sheena.

In the morning Michael rode with Erica and Sheena to the zoo, where he helped out with the many and varied duties of animal care. Erica was delighted to watch his progress. Every day he seemed to grow in confidence, and since he relieved her of many of her chores, Erica had more time to work with Sheena. In addition to the afternoon foray to Primate Island, Erica had begun to bring Java to Sheena's concrete enclosure. Unfortunately Java seemed willing to adapt to human behavior, while Sheena remained aloof and truculent in her interactions with the other chimp.

Often Nick joined them at the zoo for lunch. He'd found a salve that was fairly effective in controlling his allergic rashes, and they discovered that his worst reaction came when he was near the donkeys, reindeer and other hooved animals. Michael was quick to take advantage of his father's newfound freedom from allergy. Immediately their household increased by three hamsters and a spaniel puppy from the Dumb Friends' League.

In the evening Erica and Sheena frequently dined in the chimpproof basement room with the two Barron men.

And almost every night Nick used the key to her apartment and they made love.

Only a few factors kept them from being the settled-down family that Nick had dreamed they could be. They still maintained separate residences. And he never spent the night at her apartment. Late every night he dragged himself from her cozy bed and returned home.

On a night in early August he rose naked from her bed and went to her window, staring through the leafy branches of an elm tree at the full yellow moon. "I want to stay," he said. "I want to wake up in the morning and find you beside me."

"That does sound nice, but I promise you that mornings around here are not a pretty sight. Sheena is awake and obnoxious at dawn, and I have to leave the house at 7:30. My morning schedule is not a thrill unless you happen to be fond of Monkey Mash for breakfast."

"The thrill is being with you," he said.

"But morning is boring."

"That's what I want. To be part of all those boring, mundane, everyday routines in your life. To really live with you, and to have you living with me."

"But of course we can't. Not with Sheena. If she lived in your house, I guarantee that she would pull the leaves off every plant within two days."

He gazed at Erica, savoring her lovely nudity. They were so close, he thought, so close to being a real family. Or was he fantasizing because he wanted it so much? "I'll stay just for tonight. I could ride with you in the morning, since I'm going to spend tomorrow at the zoo, anyway."

"Don't remind me. You and Amanda are so set on the plans for this big-deal Zoo Day promotion at the end of the month that nothing else is getting accomplished."

"Zoo Day could make a major difference in her cash flow."

"And it could be a major fiasco. Honestly, Nick. All the volunteer zookeepers wearing animal costumes? That's nothing but silliness."

"You're not going to change the subject. Give me a good reason, a real reason, I shouldn't stay the night."

"Michael?"

"The boy is sixteen, Erica. He knows what's going on."

"Knowing is one thing." She unself-consciously raised her arms over her head and yawned. The gentle movement of her breasts fascinated him. "Confronting is quite another proposition."

"He can handle it."

"Are you sure? Right now, Michael thinks of me as his friend and, I hope, his mentor. Of course he knows you and I are involved, but it isn't threatening to the closeness he feels for you. Everything's working rather nicely, and I don't see a reason to mess with it."

She pursed her lips in a smug little grin, and he groaned. He could see it coming. Whenever Erica wanted to make a point, she reverted to pithy sayings, old wives' tales or anthropological observations. "Let me guess," he said. "You're going to treat me to another bit of proverbial farm wisdom, aren't you?"

"An epigram does come to mind."

Nick rolled his eyes.

"My mother always used to say to my father, 'If it isn't broken, don't fix it.' Which was, I think, very good advice. Unfortunately he seldom listened to her, and the barn was filled with crazy unworkable inventions."

"Is that why you're so unwilling to take chances? So staid and proper?"

"Me?" She sat up in bed. "Staid and proper?"

"Oh, yeah." He chuckled. She was fun to tease. He loved the way she cocked her head when she challenged him.

"After all, Erica, you're always following precise patterns. I've never known a person who is so aware of time."

"I am not. No more than the next person."

"Oh, no?" In a singsong voice he recited, "Nine o'clock in the morning, feed the camels. Ten forty-two, bring Java to the enclosure. Eleven-oh-eight, take Java back . . ."

"Consistency is important in working with animals."

"Well, I'm one male animal who wants a change of pace." He returned to the bed. "I want to stay until dawn."

Her hand rose to his chest, playfully stroking the hair above his right nipple. Their easy familiarity pleased him. Though making love to her was always a supremely special experience, they knew each other so well, so thoroughly. "Come on, Erica. Tell me to stay. Don't be a grumpy old stick in the mud."

"You sweet talker, you."

He dropped a light kiss on her forehead and growled, "I'll make it worth your while."

She yanked a curl of hair on his chest.

"Ow! What are you doing?"

"Since you say that I'm so aware of time, that makes me the expert. It isn't the right time for you to spend the night. Not yet. Someday, but not yet." She lay back, inviting him. "However, you may spend the next hour trying to change my mind."

"Is that so, Your Majesty?"

"Yes." Her eyes were full of anticipation and laughter. "I dare you."

He lowered himself beside her. "Let's make that a double dare."

She aligned her body with his. "Let's."

He eased his thigh across her legs and fitted his hand to the curve of her waist. His fingers caressed her body in ever widening circles until he touched her breast. The texture of her flesh was so soft. The creamy skin on her torso felt like smooth satin but vibrantly alive. He adored the resiliency of her breasts, the taste of them.

While he lingered over her body, her womanly scent assailed him, urging him to draw closer to her, to become one. His arousal was immediate and dynamic, an undeniable force coiling through him, stiffening his muscles. When she touched him, he felt as if he'd burst into diamond-hard fragments of pure pleasure. Yet he fought to restrain this tremendous pressure, to control his instinctive drive for release, because the greater delight came from sharing with her, seeing the ecstasy on her face, hearing the cries of passion when he had truly fulfilled her. And he, too, enjoyed the sweet agony of prolonging their lovemaking. The wait made the climax more intense.

Every night when they made love, he marveled at the level of excitement she sparked within him. Now she wriggled her thigh against his, flexed her arms around his shoulders, pressed her firm breasts against his chest. And her mouth. Oh, God, her mouth. Without speaking, she communicated a sweet, fine passion.

When he finally entered her, every fiber of his body was as taut as a steel wire, begging for relief. He gritted his teeth, forcing himself to stroke slowly, slowly within her. Her moist, slick, taut body held him in thrall. Still, he thrust with tantalizing languor. Hearing her moans of delight, feeling her legs wrap around him as she synchronized her rhythm with his. Together they moved faster, with more intensity. The friction was unbearable. His body was hot, sweating. And then they arched together, and he gave in to the miracle of release.

He caught his breath. Oh, this was so good. A gentle lassitude flowed through him, cooling the fever of his desire. Just as the tension had been all-consuming, the release was a sensation of complete, utter peace. He lay beside her, awash in tenderness.

He could spend the rest of his life with her and never cease to be amazed. He wanted to keep her with him. Always. To force the rest of the world away. To protect her.

He needed this woman for his mate and would never allow her to separate from him. How could she even think of leaving? Going to Africa? Visions of impenetrable jungle and snakes flitted across his mind, and he shuddered. Africa was far too dangerous. He would never let her go.

THE NEXT DAY at Golden Independent Zoo Erica felt an uncomfortable sense of unrest. It was nothing that could be pinpointed or explained, but she was prickly. Irritable without cause and trying to avoid human contact so she wouldn't inadvertently bite someone's head off.

Instinctively she knew she needed the comfort of an animal companion. Since Michael was with Sheena this morning, Erica went to the Reptile House, where Patty, the eight-foot-long reticulated African python, drooped lethargically over the concrete branch in her glass cage. When Erica pressed her nose against the glass, Patty flicked her tongue but didn't move.

"You look the way I feel," Erica said softly. "Kind of dragged out and droopy."

She went to the rear of the cage, carefully removed the python and arranged the thick, heavy reptile on her shoulders. She tried to handle the snakes as frequently as possible. During the snowy winter months when the zoo was closed, she and Amanda transported several of the smaller animals, including Patty, to local schools. Snakes, like all animals, required friendly contact with their keepers.

With Patty for company, Erica felt marginally better. But not congenial. Absently she patted the dry skin of the python. What on earth was the matter with her?

When she stalked away from the Reptile House with Patty still looped around her neck and arms, they were greeted by Amanda. "How nice that our Patty is having an outing this morning. She's been looking a bit down in the mouth."

"Down in the mouth?" Erica retorted. "She's a snake, Amanda. She can look open in the mouth. Or closed. But down?"

"You know what I mean." The older woman patted the snake but kept her steely gaze fastened upon Erica. "Glum. Grouchy. Unreasonably irritable."

Two children eagerly approached them, much to their parents' dismay. Amanda rapidly assured the adults. "This is Patty, the reticulated African python, and she's really quite pleasant."

The snake flicked her tongue and allowed the children to touch her. Before a crowd could gather, Erica marched quickly toward the main office.

Amanda fell into step beside her. "Nick has a marvelous idea, Erica. Since you've made it clear that you will not dress up in an animal costume for Zoo Day, would you object to a safari outfit? A pith helmet and khakis?"

"No," she snapped. "Nor will I dance around in blackface with a loincloth and spear. So don't even ask."

"Really, Erica. You're the only person who isn't getting into the spirit of this event."

"My primary concern, perhaps my only concern, is that the animals will not be subjected to unnecessary hysteria."

Amanda reached out to pet the diamond-patterned skin of the python. "I appreciate your high-minded attitude,

Erica, dear. But this is only a zoo. And I need increased revenue to function."

Erica's annoyance wilted, and guilt sprang up to take its place. She certainly hadn't meant to insult Amanda. "I know you need the money. And this is not *only* a zoo. What you've done here is provide sanctuary for animals that would otherwise have suffered. Amanda, I have absolutely no right to be critical. Your work here is dedicated and noble and good."

"Please, dear. I'm not a saint."

"I'm sorry. I don't know what's wrong with me today." Amanda held the door, and they entered the office.

"Have you heard anything about your grant?"

"From that crackpot Adventurers' Club? Hah! I'll probably never hear. And do you know what's odd? I almost don't care anymore. With every day that passes, I'm less concerned, less motivated to work for other grants. And I don't understand why."

"Don't you?" The older woman sat down behind her desk and smiled. "There's nothing wrong with being happy, Erica. I've watched you and Nick together. And Michael. You're becoming a family."

"That's exactly what Nick wants. A settled-down family."

"Is that so awful? Perhaps your own priorities are changing."

"After thirty-two years? Not likely."

It wasn't her priorities. Erica held fast to her goal of field study in Tanzania. But she realized that the routine that she and Nick had established was seductively pleasant. In her grumpy mood, she decided that all this happiness was taking the edge off her desire, making her contented and lazy. And that simply wouldn't do.

There was a shout from outside the office. "Erica?"

"In here, Nick."

What was she going to do? His idea that they were a cheery, settled-down family was incorrect and misleading. His attraction to her was blinding him, and he wasn't taking into account the type of woman she really was. Erica knew she was driven to fulfill her career goals, and that meant she wasn't the perfect woman for Nick. Not a complacent, settled-down lady, not at all. A sneaky grin played across her lips. She would see how he felt about a woman who was friendly with pythons.

Amanda read her mind. "Shall I take Patty?"

"Patty stays."

"Then I'm leaving."

Amanda and Nick met at the door. She glanced up at him and said, "Good luck."

His forehead furrowed in confusion, he stepped into the office and pivoted. "What does she mean, 'Good luck'?"

Then he saw Patty. His mouth gaped. His eyes bulged. He bolted backward and fastened himself to the wall. "My God, Erica, what the hell are you doing?"

"My job. Don't you remember? This is what I do."

She took a step toward him and watched as he forced himself under control. He peeled himself away from the wall and attempted a nonchalant gesture that was as stiff as a karate chop. His Adam's apple bobbed furiously as he gulped.

"This is Patty, a reticulated African python," she said. "Michael likes her. Actually I was going to suggest that he try a snake as a pet."

"Not in my house, he won't."

"Think of it, Nick. Wouldn't we make a charming group? You, me, Michael and our reptiles? Absolutely the ideal family unit. Or perhaps—is it possible?—perhaps I'm not the perfect mate that you keep insisting I am."

He gulped again but took a step toward her. And another. His legs moved as if he were a wooden man. With his jaw clenched he lifted his hand and touched Patty's nether regions, which coiled gracefully around Erica's arm. "She's not slimy."

"No, she's not."

Erica's intention had been to prove that she was too different, too radically different to be the one and only woman in his life. She'd wanted to show him they were mismatched, but now she was proud of him. Unreasonable fear of animals was an attitude she couldn't understand but could sympathize with. There were even some anthropological indications that fear of snakes was an instinctive rather than conditioned response. Monkeys in the wild generally reacted to snakes with frantic displays of terror.

"I'm sorry, Nick."

"No need. This is probably good for me. Facing this little phobia, dealing with it."

"Would you like to hold Patty?"

"Not on your life."

She turned away from him, took Patty into the back of the office and carefully placed her in a snake bag. Then she returned to the outer office, where Nick watched her warily.

"Patty isn't going to get out, is she?"

"Not a chance."

"I'm assuming you had a reason for this fun little episode."

She nodded. "But I'm not sure what it is. Nick, I'm happy in our relationship. And I guess it goes without saying that the physical part is wonderful. But there's something about us that is making me crazy."

"Me, too." He perched on the edge of Amanda's desk.

"Really?" She took a position beside him. "What is it?"

"We're starting to feel like a family."

"But I thought that was what you wanted, Nick."

"My idea of the perfect family, as you know, is a stable, settled-down-in-one-place thing. Like I said last night, I don't want to leave your bed in the middle of the night. I want you and me and Michael and the dozens of pets he's bound to accumulate to be safe and secure in one house. One home."

"But that's not my perfect family portrait. Not at all. I envision a globe-trotting family unit. With freedom to grow and develop."

Nick slipped his arm around her shoulder, and she had to admit he was more comfort than Patty the python.

"What's the solution?"

"Erica, my fine beautiful lady, I wish I knew."

Perhaps there was no answer, but Erica was determined to search. She would observe their responses, catalog them and reach a conclusion. After all, there were explanations for all types of behavior. Except, perhaps, for love.

9

LOVE.

A few days later Erica sat at her desk in the vacant chimp enclosure at the zoo. She'd finished recording another bonding incident between Java and Lenny, had set aside her pen and was thinking about love.

Of course love was out of the question, absolutely taboo, incongruous with a temporary commitment. Both she and Nick had been cautious in their declarations to each other. Though they'd shared a remarkable closeness, neither one of them had said, "I love you."

Guiltily Erica realized she'd been thinking it.

At night when they lay in bed together, she would think "love" but would never say the words. Was Nick doing the same thing? Why? There was nothing magical in the statement. People said it all the time.

She tore a page from her journal and picked up her pen. She would inventory her feelings, write them as if they were observations of a peculiar primate phenomenon.

She noted, "The female exhibits caring behavior toward the male. And he reciprocates. When she is near him, her heartbeat accelerates. They both enjoy their sexual interludes. She laughs more frequently when they are together. Her spoken communication is more animated, excited. Likewise, the male responds to her, touching her frequently and with great familiarity. Possible conclusion: they are in love."

She tore out another page and scrawled the word "however" across the top. "However, the female is a highly motivated individual. Her goal is to work in Africa, which means she will ultimately desert the male and forsake the bonds between them. The male wants to settle down, engage in nesting rituals. The female wishes to soar. Alone? No, not necessarily alone."

Her pen fell to the desktop. If there were anyone in the world she wished to share her life with, it was Nick. If only he would come with her to Africa.

Again she wrote. "Though the male appears to take the female's ambitions seriously, he is dedicated to his own life-style. Conclusion: . . . there is no conclusion. Further observation is required."

Erica leaned back in her chair and rubbed her eyes. Perhaps she was creating a problem where none existed. After all, she still hadn't heard from the Adventurers' Club, and she had the awful feeling they would turn down her grant, anyway. The issue of her African journey might not arise for years, and she probably ought to relax and enjoy herself in the never ending meanwhile—a state of limbo that was made bearable, pleasurable, in fact, by the hours she spent with Nick.

She checked her wristwatch. Three-oh-eight. It was time for Sheena's daily foray to the island. Where was Michael? For that matter, where was Sheena? She closed her journal and hurried up the hill to the office.

"Amanda? Have you seen Michael or Sheena?"

"I thought Sheena was with you. Nick came by about half an hour ago and picked her up."

"What? Did he say where he was going?"

Amanda shook her head.

Erica raced from the office. Nick hadn't made arrangements to take Sheena. What was going on? Michael would probably know what his father intended to do. But where was Michael? She ran down to Primate Island. After peering through the branches, she spied the young man squatting behind a shrub. "Michael!"

Slowly and carefully, so as not to disturb Java, he lifted his arm and waved.

"Michael Barron, you get back over here. Right now."

Obediently but reluctantly, he crept from the island and forded the moat. Erica noticed that he wasn't rushing and his expression was recalcitrant and guilty. His sneaker-clad feet were still in the stream when she demanded, "Where's Sheena? What's going on?"

"I guess Dad didn't find you, huh?"

"I guess not."

"This was a bad idea. Real bad."

She grabbed his hand and yanked him onto the shore. "I assume that your father has taken off somewhere with Sheena. Tell me where. And why."

"To Barron's. There are these, you know, special kids coming to Barron's this afternoon, and he thought they might get turned on by meeting Sheena."

Erica was furious. How dared he! Why had she presumed that Nick cared one whit about her career? Obviously he didn't take her seriously.

"You're mad," Michael observed.

"Yes. I am mad."

"At me?"

He looked at her with puppy-dog eyes, and Erica reined in her anger. It wasn't fair to take it out on Michael. "I'm not mad at you. It's just that your father is disregarding all the efforts I am making with Sheena. How could he encourage her to play with children? He knows I'm trying so hard to integrate Sheena into the tribe of chimps."

"*We're* trying hard," Michael ventured. "You *and* me."

"That's right." She patted his shoulder. "Michael, this isn't your fault, and it will work out. No problem. Would you feed the chimps? And tell Amanda that I'll be gone."

"Okay. But what are you going to do?"

"I am going to Barron's," she said quietly. "I will find your father. And I will break both of his arms."

"Listen, Dad didn't mean any harm. Really. And we can fix it with Sheena. I mean, she's really doing a lot better. Like yesterday? When she let Java touch her? She's going to be okay."

Erica studied the young man's expression. Though his eyes were the same gold-flecked brown as his father's, Michael's gaze betrayed a vulnerability she had seldom seen in Nick's.

"Michael, I want you to know that no matter what happens between your father and me, you'll always have a place with me here at the zoo. You're very talented in working with the animals and—"

"But it does," he interrupted. "It does matter what happens between you and Dad."

The vulnerability in his eyes changed to fear—a justifiable fear. She couldn't promise him a happy ending for this story, a final commitment to his father.

"It matters, Erica. I really like you."

"I know, Michael. It matters to me, too." Her features softened. "We'll talk tomorrow, okay?"

"Yeah, okay. But can I call you tonight?"

"You certainly may." She took his hands and squeezed them. "You're special to me. Not only because you're the best assistant I've ever had, but also because I like you as a friend."

"Thanks." He treated her to a handsome Barron smile.

She swiftly took her leave, dashed to her car and headed into Denver.

On the periphery of her mind she'd known that more was involved in her temporary commitment to Nick than the two of them, but it hadn't seemed important until now. While she and Nick acted out their definitions of family and structured their relationship, Michael stood helpless in the wings, waiting for the outcome. What would he feel if she left for Africa? Deserted? Abandoned?

Though she didn't perceive a mother-son bonding between them, she couldn't be sure of the role Michael had assigned her. It was possible that working together at the zoo every day was too intense an association. Perhaps Michael needed to be spending more time with kids his own age. Yet he never complained about the long hours, and his enthusiasm grew daily.

When she pulled up at a stoplight, her hands fidgeted on the steering wheel, and she read the bumper sticker on the car ahead of her. I Brake for Animals.

"So do I," Erica muttered. Never would she consciously harm an animal. And yet she had neglected Michael's feelings. It seemed certain that he would be hurt if her relationship with his father came to an end. Temporary commitments could be dangerous.

By the time she parked in the Barron's employee lot, her anger at Nick had paled in comparison to her concern for his son. Still, she slammed her car door. Maybe she would break only one of his arms.

After asking around, she discovered him in a pavilion in the gardens, sitting in the center of a ring of children. Special children, Michael had said. And Erica understood. Three were in wheelchairs. Others wore bandages and splints. There were four other adults, sitting outside their circle. Sheena, on her leash, was in the middle.

Erica stood quietly, leaning against a white wooden pillar, and watched. The sunlight shining through the latticework roof made bright dappled splotches on the children's faces.

"Sheena is not a monkey," Nick explained. "She's an ape, and she is very much like you and me. If you poke at her, she'll be hurt or she'll get angry. She might poke back. Or she might want to run away and hide."

The solemn nods from some of the children tugged at Erica's heart. They knew what it meant to be hurt.

"What does she look like?" asked a little boy whose milky-blue eyes stared sightlessly into the distance. "May I touch her?"

Nick brought the chimp close to the blind child and directed his small hand to Sheena's hunched shoulder. The boy stroked her, outlining the shape of her ears with his finger and exploring the little ape's body. Throughout Sheena stood still, peering at the child. "She's got long arms," the boy said. "But I bet she's pretty."

Sheena enfolded the boy in her long, hairy arms and planted a sloppy chimp kiss on his face.

He giggled. "I love you, too, Sheena."

Nick moved patiently around the circle, allowing each child to interact with Sheena.

"She can hang upside down by her toes," Nick said. "And she's very strong."

"Like King Kong?" asked a girl in a wheelchair.

"Well, that's not a very true story about apes. Most of the time an ape would never attack a man. And they never ever get as big as King Kong."

"But they're very naughty. I saw a movie about chimpanzees, and they always got into trouble. They were worse than kids."

Sheena noticed a restlessness in Sheena and decided that it was time to join the group. "Chimps and kids aren't the only creatures that get into trouble," she said, favoring

Nick with a quick scowl. "Sometimes grown-ups are naughty, too."

She took Sheena's hand. "My name is Erica, and I work at Golden Independent Zoo. Sheena lives at my apartment."

"I betcha it's a mess."

"You're right. It is. Now do you have any questions?"

"Does Sheena do any tricks?"

"She's not a circus chimp, and I haven't trained her. But she does like to play tricks." She told them about Sheena's escape through the window. "She was very clever to figure out how to open the window locks. And very naughty to run off all by herself."

"Did she get a spanking?"

"I never spank Sheena. And that's for two reasons. First, because her behavior is natural to her. My idea of right and wrong doesn't count because I'm not a chimp. Second, I don't ever spank her because she is so very strong. If she decided to spank back, we'd have a royal battle."

As if to illustrate, Sheena bounced up and down on her leash, making vigorous pant-hooting noises.

"What's she saying?"

"Sheena can't talk the way we can, but that noise is a signal that chimps use to call one another in the jungle. And I'm afraid it also means that it's time for us to go."

After Sheena made her round of farewells, Erica led her away. Nick joined them.

"Am I going to get a spanking?" he asked.

"You should! Your behavior was irresponsible. And you know better. You know not to take Sheena, but you did it, anyway." She glared at his grinning face. "Really, Nick! At least have the decency to look ashamed of yourself."

"I'm not sorry. Those kids deserve something more than a ride on the carousel. Did you see how excited they were?"

"Yes, I saw."

Beside a weeping willow she hoisted Sheena to her hip, gaining a firm grip on the chimp before they moved into the crowded midway at the amusement park. Nick had been wrong to take Sheena without telling her. But his instincts to offer a special surprise to the children couldn't be faulted.

"Erica, if I'd told you I wanted to take Sheena to meet some special kids, would you have agreed to let her go?"

She bit her lower lip. "I'd like to think I would have. But, honestly, I don't know."

After watching Sheena's performance and seeing how much the children enjoyed her, she would have agreed. But that was hindsight. It was equally likely that she would have refused.

For the second time that day Erica faced the possibility that she was less than perceptive when it came to relations with other human beings. Her attitude was not unlike Sheena's problems with the other chimps on the island. They were both misfits, out of step with their own kind.

No, she thought, it wasn't the same thing. She was making very conscious, considered choices. Limiting Sheena's contact with human beings was important to her research. And the research was her life. Did Nick understand that? This was the first time his actions indicated that he didn't take her career seriously.

All things considered, however, she wasn't unhappy with what he'd done. It spoke well of him that his sensitivity toward the needs of the children had overruled his common sense, and she hoped that her own errors in judgment might be in the same direction. Knowing the right decision was so difficult, especially when feelings got in the way.

They came out of the garden area to the colorful, crowded midway. When Erica headed toward the parking lot, he caught her arm. "Come to my office."

"I don't think so, Nick. I was pretty furious with you. Now I'm feeling like the Wicked Witch of the West. It's better that I have some time alone."

"Please, Erica. I have a reason."

"No. I told you how I was feeling, and I want you to respect that." Under her breath she added, "Even if you don't respect my career decisions."

"Okay," he said with a shrug. "This is kind of important. But I can see you're in one of your stubborn, I-want-to-be-alone moods, so forget it."

"How is this important?"

"You have to come to my office to find out." He gave her a little kiss on the forehead, scratched Sheena behind the ear and walked away. "See you later."

Erica rolled her eyes and called after him. "Can't you just tell me?"

"Nope." He kept walking.

A frustrating moment of indecision: Should she go with him? Or stay by herself? Oh, hell, she could be by herself later. "Wait, Nick! I'm coming with you."

She caught up with him and fell into step, keeping her gaze straight ahead. She didn't want to see what she knew would be a smug expression on his face.

In his voice she could almost hear the smirk when he said, "Curiosity got the best of you, huh?"

"I guess I do need to talk to you." She adjusted Sheena's weight on her hip. "About Michael."

"What about him? There's nothing wrong, is there?"

"Not yet. But he did seem awfully upset today when I threatened to break both of your arms."

Nick laughed with relief. "Is that all?"

"Not really. We do need to talk seriously about the impact of our relationship on your son. Today I realized how much our indecision could hurt him. He's developing an attachment to me that has nothing to do with our work. Almost like he wants to think of me as his mother. But he can't because you and I aren't making commitments."

"Ouch," Nick said.

They entered Kiddy Land, moving at a fairly swift pace to avoid the inevitable crowd of curious children who wanted to touch Sheena.

"Is that all you have to say?" Erica glanced up at him. "I tell you that your son is undergoing inappropriate bonding behavior, and all you have to say is 'ouch'?"

"That about sums it up."

"I might as well be talking to Sheena."

Sheena peered into her face and hooted.

"Nick, human beings are supposed to be able to communicate."

He led her down the tulip-lined path to his windmill-shaped office. "First, let me show you what I have in here."

They entered his cool, silent office. A few weeks ago, as a joke, Erica and Michael had rigged up three separate tape players so that when Nick entered his office, he was assailed with an earsplitting blast of music—Mick Jagger and the Rolling Stones.

Nick went to his desk. "Before I came to the park, I stopped by your apartment to pick up one of Sheena's leashes. The postman was there, and he gave me your mail."

He held out an envelope.

Erica removed Sheena's leash and allowed her to roam freely through the office before she took the envelope and saw the return address: Adventurers' Club.

"Oh, my God," she said. "This is it."

"Yes, it is."

Erica distractedly watched Sheena bound to the half-size refrigerator and make her "good food" hoot. Nick responded by opening the door. In a flash Sheena grabbed two apples.

Erica was aware that these simple activities were going on, but she was distanced from them. In her hand she held the future, her future, and she was both terrified and excited.

Nick returned to her side and waved his fingers in front of her face. "Earth to Erica. Do you read me?"

"What? Oh, yes, of course."

She started to open the envelope but froze again.

"Well?" he questioned. "Aren't you going to open it?"

"What if it's a rejection?" She stared blankly past him. "Oh, Nick, you don't know how many times I've gone through this. Holding the envelope in my hand, wishing and hoping with all my heart. Then inside is the refusal. Always nicely phrased, but a refusal nonetheless."

Gently he held her, and she gratefully subsided into his arms. There was comfort within his embrace, but not protection. He couldn't rescue her from the contents of this letter. It was written—either an acceptance or a rejection—and the letters would not magically reform themselves. All alone, Erica had ventured out on a limb, making her proposal, and Nick couldn't help her. No one could help her.

He stroked her trembling shoulders. "It's all right, Erica."

"I have only one more grant proposal out besides this one. What if this is a rejection, Nick?"

"You'll never know unless you open it."

"Right." She moved away from his embrace, ripped open the envelope and yanked out a single sheet of paper.

Her knees gave out, and she sank into a chair, unable to face the possibility that she had failed again. Her eyes refused to focus on the words of the letter. Paragraphs. Lines. A salutation: Dear Erica Swanson.

She held the letter out to Nick. "Would you please read this out loud?"

Taking the letter from her, he read, " 'Your presentation and slides were most interesting, and we have given your proposal serious consideration.' "

"It's a rejection," she moaned. She was familiar enough with the phrasing of failure. First there would be the kind words about how admirable she was, then the inevitable regrets. She flopped back in the chair and closed her eyes. "Oh, well, better luck next time. And the next. And the next. Dammit, Nick. How long does this have to go on? How many million proposals must I file before someone gives me a chance?"

" 'The Adventurers' Club,' " he read aloud, " 'has taken the final decision to support you. In three weeks, on the first of September, funds will be made available for your trip to Tanzania and a one year's stay to establish a research facility.' "

He knelt beside the chair where she sat. "They're going to fund you, Erica."

"Oh."

Had she heard him correctly? It couldn't be. She wanted to hear an acceptance so very much that she must be imagining his words. A sound like the roaring of the ocean surf echoed in her ears.

"There's more here," he said. "About the vital nature of ethology and primatology and man's relation to the apes. And protecting the natural habitat. In addition to your research, they want you to look into possible political means of establishing vast national parks in the rain forest areas."

"Oh."

He took her hand in his. "It's your dream come true."

"Are you sure?" She snatched the letter from him and read it herself. They would fund her. Completely. They believed in her, supported her. She had succeeded.

"Erica? Are you all right? You look pale."

"It's an acceptance."

He laughed. "Yes, Erica, it is."

"I did it!" She burst from the chair like a skyrocket, exploding in a loud, triumphant whoop. She bounced up and down, giving wild hoots of celebration. "I did it! It's happening! I'm going to Africa!"

Nick stood, and she flung herself into his arms, wrapping her arms around his neck and her legs around his waist and clinging to him like a chimp. She kissed him hard and bounded away, running to Sheena and hugging her. "I'm going to see all your relatives in Africa, Sheena. I'm going to live with them for a year."

The little ape bared her teeth in a wide grin.

Erica grinned back, then ran to Nick. "I leave in three weeks? Oh, my gosh, I have so much to do."

"You can handle it."

He watched as she paced and laughed and shouted. There was a frenzied aura of excitement in her, giving her eyes a sparkle and her hair and skin a sheen. On and on she chattered about packing and shopping and making arrangements with Amanda. Lord, she was beautiful. Maybe a little crazy, but beautiful.

He smiled. Though she hadn't once considered what would happen to them, to their relationship, he could forgive her. It wasn't very often that dreams came true.

"I'm happy for you, Erica. Should we go out tonight and celebrate?"

"Yes. You and me and Michael. And I want to eat steak. Not Monkey Mash, not fruit salad, but a giant, juicy steak."

"How's the food in Tanzania?"

"Not bad in the more civilized locations. But I'll probably be roughing it, cooking for myself."

"Hold it right there, lady. You are not planning to be completely isolated in the snake-infested jungle of an emerging Third World nation, are you?"

"Didn't you listen to my presentation? I'll be in association with the other established groups, but I plan to set up an outpost for studying the migratory habits of courtship, bonding and mating. And, of course, my proposal includes funding for one full-time assistant and one half-time." She whirled around and faced him. "You're not worried about me, are you?"

He beheld the dark-eyed woman standing before him. Though she wasn't big or muscular, she radiated strength. With arms akimbo and feet planted firmly apart, she looked as if she could take on the world. But could she? Of course he was concerned and anxious. He was worried that she wouldn't come back to him.

He stretched toward her, touching her forearm. Static electricity sparked between them, and he withdrew his hand, sensing that their separation had already begun. In her mind, he thought, she was halfway to Tanzania, a world away from him. "I'll miss you."

"Oh, my God, Nick. I'm going to be leaving you."

He nodded. "It appears so."

"Our temporary relationship . . ." Something crumbled inside her, and the very foundations of her happiness trembled. This should have been the most perfect, proudest moment in her life, the pinnacle of all her work, study and planning. Her goals were about to come to fruition. Yet a deep sorrow obscured her brilliant future.

Her eyes swam with tears, and her vision of Nick seemed hazy and unfocused, as if he were fading, becoming indistinct.

All of a sudden she didn't want to go.

Erica held out her arms to him and leaned into his embrace. His body fitted so beautifully with hers. Was it possible that she was going to leave him? Whatever it was that had grown between them was fine and good. She couldn't let it go, push it away.

She wanted it all. Her career and her relationship with Nick. But that wasn't possible.

Her head dropped against him and she sobbed. Clinging to him in the silent office, she cried and cried. Yet all her tears couldn't wash away the bone-deep despair she felt.

"How can I leave you, Nick?"

"We knew this was coming. If not today, then tomorrow or next week. This possibility has always been with us."

"Come with me?" She tilted her tear-streaked face imploringly toward his. "You could be my assistant. And Michael, too. We'd have a wonderful time, an adventure. Please, Nick. Please say you'll come with me."

"I can't."

"Sure, you can. At least for the winter. Barron's closes in the winter, anyway, doesn't it?"

"Yes. We're only open during weekends in September, then the park is closed for six months."

"You see," she said brightly as she wiped away her tears. "Then you'll come. Oh, Nick, it will be so good. I can't wait to show you—"

"No, Erica," he said firmly.

"But it's possible. Sure, it will take some arranging, but you can do it."

"This is your dream, lady. Not mine."

"Oh, please, Nick. If you come with me, everything will be perfect."

"I don't want to."

His words stung like a slap, a physical blow, and she recoiled. Was this the rejection she'd sensed? That he really didn't care for her?

Still staring into his face, she backed away from him, shaking her head. No, this couldn't be true. This wasn't happening. The feelings she had for him, feelings that very much resembled love, were too strong. They couldn't be one-sided. He must care something for her. He must. She couldn't have been that far off track.

Maybe she hadn't heard him correctly. She'd misunderstood the letter; maybe this was the same thing. "Nick?"

"I don't want to go with you, Erica."

Was this goodbye? Erica lowered her eyes, exhausted. Her life had been building to this moment. Since her childhood when she'd read and reread *National Geographic*, to her first trip to the Gombe River, she'd imagined a life devoted to study. She'd dreamed of this as the ultimate freedom with no responsibility other than her work.

Now the dream felt empty. She gathered up Sheena, fastened the chimp's leash to her collar and walked from Nick's office into the garish sunlight. Alone. Except for Sheena, she was alone.

10

ERICA IGNORED the persistent ringing of the telephone in her apartment, finally taking the receiver off the hook. She fed Sheena and escorted the little chimp to her bedroom, where toys littered the floor and two hammocks dangled from the ceiling. Usually Sheena preferred sleeping on the futon or on the Formica floor, but tonight she leaped into a hammock and rolled into a ball with her feet above her head.

"Well," Erica said, "you don't seem any the worse for your experience today. SOS, huh? Same old Sheena?"

Sheena didn't answer; she was occupied with an intense study of the toes on her left foot.

Erica checked the wire mesh over the windows and scanned the room for potential hazards that Sheena might have hidden for after-hours playtime. The room seemed safe, and Erica turned out the light. "Sleep tight."

Then Erica went to her own bedroom. Still dressed in her zoo uniform, she sprawled on the bed. Had this day been the same length as every other day? It seemed like an eternity since this morning, and she knew these twenty-four long hours had wrought incredible changes in her life. She wasn't the same woman she'd been at dawn. Her waking thoughts this morning had been of Nick, of his body lying beside her. And, of course, she'd thought of the grant during the day. Not a single day went by that she didn't think of the grant possibilities and her future in Africa.

Now she'd lost one. And won the other. She was elated and utterly depressed. Sadder but wiser?

She turned on the radio beside her bed, plugged in her headphones and turned the volume on high. The throbbing beat of rock music with indistinguishable, repetitive lyrics pounded through her brain. Oh, yeah, oh, yeah, oh, yeah. Oh, baby, oh, baby, oh, baby. Louder. She wanted the primal electric chords to paralyze her brain, to chase away all coherent thought, to relax her until her mind was completely absorbed. Oh, yeah, oh, baby.

"Oh, Nick." She turned off the music.

On the shelves that hung on the wall her collection of glass animals glittered. One animal for every year. Her hurts and her triumphs sparkled.

In her sixteenth year she'd fallen in love for the first time. Half a lifetime ago. That was the year she'd actually started her collection, purchasing a tiny glass rose to symbolize the occasion when her boyfriend had given her flowers. She touched the figurines. A lion, a bear, a mouse and chimps. Several little people: one carried an umbrella, another wore a sombrero, another was playing tennis. And symbols of various events, like a boat, an airplane, a daisy and a wishing well.

It seemed that her collection, the events of her life, were balanced between career decisions and a continual seeking for love. Now, she thought, the two had collided. Her career had catapulted into high gear. Her love? She couldn't even call it love. All she'd had was a temporary commitment, and that was withering, painfully dying as, by its very nature, it must.

"I am not going to cry again," she vowed.

Gathering her robe and nightgown, she went to the bathroom, pushed aside the clear shower curtain and turned on the tub faucets. It wasn't often that she indulged in the hedonistic pleasure of a long soak. Showers were quick, and her hectic schedule required that she bathe as speedily as possible.

Tonight, however, she wished to steep in water that was as hot as she could stand it. Even before she'd peeled off her uniform, steam had fogged the bathroom mirror. She swizzled jasmine-scented oil in the water and eased herself into the hot tub.

Gradually she got used to the heat, allowing the scented water to swirl around her legs and over her tummy, warming her, relaxing the ache of tension.

She let her head loll back against the white porcelain tub and breathed deeply of the floral aroma. Comforting. The heat of the water penetrated her pores. Calming. Erica's mother had always suggested a nice hot bath for whatever ailed. When little Erica received a bad grade on a math test, when a spring snow destroyed her garden, when she and her boyfriend broke up, her mother would say, "How about a nice hot bath? Then we'll talk about it." Even if they didn't get around to the talking part, Erica always felt better.

There must be some mysterious, therapeutic value in bathing. She trailed her finger across the water's surface. In Tanzania there would be no long, soothing baths. After she set up her outpost camp, water would have to be hauled from a stream and boiled over a fire. And the nights, she thought, would be beautifully still. No traffic. No telephones. No television. No rock 'n' roll music for her in Tanzania. Instead, she would be serenaded by howling hyenas, hooting owls and breezes stirring the lush canopy of trees. Nick would love the silence of the jungle.

"Damn." She made a rippling splash in the bathwater. Nick wouldn't be with her.

She heard a tapping at the bathroom door. "Erica? Are you all right?"

"Nick?" She caught her breath. "What are you doing here?"

"I have something to say to you. May I come in?"

"No, you may not." She slid down until the water was up to her chin. "Go away."

"Thank you," he said, and opened the bathroom door.

With a swift yank Erica pulled the shower curtain across the tub. It was clear plastic and gave virtually no shelter. Though Nick was slightly distorted, she could still see him. And he could see her. Strangely, she was embarrassed. This was a man who had shared the most intimate secrets of her body. He had seen her naked a hundred times, but now she wanted to hide. Crossing her arms over her breasts, she peeked over the edge of the tub. "Go away, Nick."

"The hell I will."

"I don't want to see you."

"Well, you're going to have to explain yourself to somebody. And it's better to me than my son." His voice was sharp. "You remember Michael, don't you? You work with him every day at the zoo, and you promised to talk to him tonight."

She groaned. This afternoon she'd resolved to be more aware of Michael's feelings, and she'd already betrayed her promise. "You're right. As soon as you leave, I'll call him."

Through the clear shower curtain she saw him lean against the sink and fold his arms across his chest. "By the way, Erica, I told him that you'd received your grant, and that damn fool kid wants to go with you. Naturally I informed him that was out of the question."

"He can't? Or you don't want him to?"

"Of course I don't want him to. But there is also a pretty important reason he can't take off for the jungle. He's only sixteen and has another year of high school to complete."

"I agree with that, Nick, and I will tell Michael. It's important that he finish school."

"Thanks a whole lot. I thought for a few minutes that I was going to lose both of you to the chimps."

"If you've said what you have to say, I would appreciate it if you'd leave, Nick."

"But I don't want to leave." He reached for the shower curtain.

"Don't touch that," she said. "Leave, Nick. There's really no point in staying."

"Why? Because I don't want to go to Africa as your spear carrier? You set up pretty strict rules, don't you? Either it's your way one hundred percent, or it's nothing at all."

"You said you don't want to be with me," she snapped.

"I said I don't want to go to Tanzania. And I don't. Hanging around in a jungle, watching the apes, is your idea of a good time. Not mine."

"Oh, yeah? Then why did you go searching for Atlantis?"

"It was a slow weekend."

He turned away from the tub and rested his hand on the doorknob, but he didn't leave. "Actually I consider that expedition to be my great adventure. At least once in every man's life he should be able to take off on an impossible quest."

"Why not twice?"

"Because it only takes one time around to prove that there's nothing there. And then you move on."

"This is different," she insisted. "I learned from my father and his crackpot schemes not to chase the impossible. My expedition is scientific, and I will find something. Maybe it will be only a footnote in an anthropology textbook, but I will add something to the scope of human knowledge."

"I know that, Erica. And I'm glad for you. Really damn glad that you're going to do this. But it's not my life."

He took a deep breath and turned back toward the tub. "You know my dream as well as I know yours. I want a quiet home and a comfortable easy chair. Soft music. A good book. Maybe a fire on the hearth. I want to be able to draw my family around me, to take care of them, to protect them."

"I guess we're different."

"But that doesn't mean that either of us is right or wrong. We have three more weeks before you leave. I want to spend that time with you."

"Why? Your dream includes a committed relationship, and you know that isn't possible with me."

"My dream can wait."

"No," she protested weakly. "We'll only hurt each other."

"You promised me, Erica." He knelt beside the tub and pushed aside the shower curtain. "You agreed to a temporary commitment, which, by your own definition, means that you'll spend time with me while you can."

"Surely you aren't going to hold me to that."

"Oh, yes." He nodded. "I am. I know that you're a slave to responsibility, that you don't make commitments lightly. And I damn well intend to hold you to our agreement."

"What if I refuse?"

"You won't."

She glared at him. How dared he bring up their temporary commitment as if it had been signed, sealed and notarized! "You're so sure of yourself, aren't you?"

"No, I'm sure of you. You're the little girl who sprained her ankle jumping out of a barn loft rather than back out of a dare. And you're the woman who promised to spend time with me."

She drew back her hand and splashed bathwater at him.

He rose to his feet. "I'll be waiting for you, Erica. After you've calmed down."

He left her fuming in the bathtub and went into the front room to settle in a battered chair. He didn't bother to turn on a light. The darkness was soothing to the turmoil he felt inside, and he forced his mind to go blank, to find a still point of silence. An inner space.

"Dammit." His confusion erupted. He'd known that she would be leaving, but until it was imminent, he had avoided thinking about it. He would not let their relationship end. Temporary or not. He would hold it, make her see reason.

He heard the bathroom door open. In her flannel robe she padded past him to the kitchen telephone. He watched her dial. "Hello," she said. "Michael?"

There was a pause.

"Thank you. And I want you to know that everything is all right, everything that matters. Listen, Michael, since I'm going to be leaving, that means my research at the zoo will have to end unless I can find someone to take over. I could check with the local universities for students, but you've already developed a rapport with the chimps, and I would rather have you continue the work. Are you interested?"

She paused, and he saw her smile.

"Yes, you'd be the boss. But this shouldn't interfere with your schoolwork. The job is a big responsibility."

She nodded.

"Good. We'll talk more in the morning."

She furrowed her forehead after she recradled the telephone receiver. It probably would have been better to ask Nick before mentioning the research possibility to his son. But Michael really was good with the animals. If he continued, it would be the perfect solution.

"What is a big responsibility?" Nick asked.

She jumped. "You're still here. Were you eavesdropping?"

"You might say that. I would prefer to think that I was looking out for my own best interests. And I gather that you've asked my son to take over your research at the zoo."

"Yes."

"Not that it would stop either one of you if I disagreed, but you have my blessing. It's been good for Michael to work at the zoo. Teaches him responsibility."

"And he's talented," she put in.

"Come on, Erica." He crossed the room until he stood before her. "You're always saying that, but how talented does somebody have to be to feed and clean up after an animal?"

"Just as talented as somebody who raises plants."

"Wait a minute," he said. "Are you equating the very delicate plant splicing that I do with slopping the buffalo?"

"Precisely. Some people would only throw food at the buffalo and get out of the pen. Michael notices things. Like the buffalo didn't eat well the day before. Or their coats are matted. Or they're limping. And he takes care of them. So the buffalo are healthy and happy. Like your plants."

"And that's a talent?"

"You bet it is. Some people are born animal lovers."

"Speaking of which." He spoke brashly with an assurance he didn't feel. "There's a party I have to go to tomorrow night. It's being put on by the advertising agency that handles Barron's publicity."

"And what does this have to do with animals?"

"The party is to promote a new perfume called Safari."

Erica gave a dry laugh. Her memories of safari-type expeditions didn't equate with a scent that someone would purposely want to emulate.

"Actually," he said, "I wanted to take Amanda because I thought she might get some good ideas for her Zoo Day promotion, but she insisted that I take you. I'll pick you up at eight o'clock tomorrow night."

His invitation lay before her like a challenge, and Erica had never walked away from a battle in her life. "Eight o'clock will be fine."

"Good." He leaned forward as if to kiss her, but instead he grasped her hand for a firm shake. "I'm glad that you'll be honoring the terms of our temporary commitment."

Before she could retort, he went to the door.

"Nick? What shall I wear?"

He turned the knob. "The invitation said jungle dress."

ERICA HAD SEVERAL CHOICES for appropriate jungle attire. The most spectacular was a massive, circular Masai ceremonial necklace, but she knew it really should be worn bare breasted, which seemed a bit much. Or she could wrap herself in a simple sarong and add a turban. And there was a wonderful, bright tunic she'd purchased in Nairobi. Finally she opted for comfort and slipped into her wide khaki shorts and matching shirt. To top off the outfit, she added a stained, battered pith helmet.

She'd spent most of the day trying to decide what the terms of their temporary commitment meant and why he wanted to continue seeing her. Finally she'd accepted that they had three weeks. A lot could happen in three weeks. In that time it was just barely possible that she could convince him to come with her.

When she opened the door for Nick, she was confronted with a foot-tall mask painted in black, red and white. "Boola! Boola!"

"Very nice," she said. "But not authentic."

"B'wana lady is pretty smart. This was made in Taiwan."

"And boola is something they say at Harvard football games, not in Tanzania."

"Yeah? Well, maybe I'm a member of the Preppy tribe."

She laughed. It was good to laugh with him. Their laughter brought balance to their uneasy relationship.

And she was glad to see that his outfit was also casual—a pale blue, tie-dyed dashiki-type shirt and white cotton trousers with sandals.

"You look good," he said. "Is that the type of clothing you'll wear in Tanzania?"

"Pretty much." The mention of her trip sounded a sour note, and Erica wished she'd been more frivolous in her choice of dress. "So where is this event?"

"Downtown."

They whisked off in his Mercedes sedan. Erica kept trying to avoid mentioning her grant, but it was impossible, especially when Nick asked leading questions. "Did you tell Amanda? What does she think?"

"Happy for me, but sorry that I'm leaving the zoo. And I'm sorry, too. The zoo has been a real learning experience for me, both in taking care of the animals and in watching Amanda. She's a remarkable lady. I've learned a lot about compassion and determination from her."

"As if you needed lessons on determination!" He chuckled. "That's like teaching a hawk to fly."

"Are you saying I'm stubborn?"

"Has anyone ever told you otherwise?"

She didn't need to think for even a second. "No. From the time I was little, my mother used to give me a hard time about being so stubborn. 'Erica,' she'd say, 'you've got to learn the meaning of give and take. You're never going to find yourself a husband if you keep up . . .'" Her words trailed away.

More and more often she was finding her mother's bits of wisdom to be true. She was never going to find a mate.

"She was wrong," Nick said. "You were married once."

"Yes, I was." But not to the man she wanted for her mate.

They parked in the lot beneath the hotel and joined a colorful throng bound for the safari party.

Right away Erica noticed that she was the most plainly clad woman in the group. Even the other women who had opted for banana republic khaki had decorated the plain garments with yards and yards of colorful scarves or high slit skirts or flashy jewelry. But it was the abundance of sarongs that made Erica feel drab—the sarongs and the wild headdresses with feathers and sequins and long ropes of beads.

"This looks formal," she muttered to Nick.

"It's this group of people. Party-goers. Some of these ladies dress up to go to the supermarket." He removed her pith helmet and kissed the top of her head. "You look great."

Really? She wondered. Either he was playing the part of a polite escort or true love was blind. Not love, she reminded herself firmly. That particular word was not part of their vocabulary. Like, she amended. True like is blind?

As soon as she entered the ballroom, Erica knew she was in the wrong place. Amid the glittering human refinery and a lush display of tropical plants were animals, caged animals who paced nervously behind iron bars. A whimpering hyena. A skinny, spotted leopard. A fat black leopard. And two furry black gibbons with sad, white faces.

On a platform at the far end of the room, a reggae band played their exotic rhythms, which were Caribbean rather than African. Which was typical, Erica thought. Nothing at this party was authentic. It was all an ugly sham.

Nick leaned close to her. "I'm sorry, Erica. I didn't know it would be like this. Let me greet a few people, then we'll leave."

"Those are gibbons," she said. "They're apes, like the chimps, but gibbons are monogamous and more arboreal in their habits."

"Monogamous?"

"Yes, they mate for life, and their family groups aren't very different from human families."

One gibbon sat morosely in a corner of the cramped cage, plucking at the dull fur on his leg. The other rattled the bars and cried. The varying tonal inflections of her song would have been beautiful in the jungle, but here in the city at a silly party the sounds were tragic. Who could be amused by this? The animals didn't belong here.

Erica swallowed hard. Her first inclination was to free these animals, go gather them to her and take them to the zoo, where they would be treated decently. But it wasn't her right to demand. These cats and apes, even the raggedy-looking hyena, must belong to someone who rented them out for parties, some idiot, and this was the individual she needed to threaten. "Who's in charge of this affair?"

"Miles Patterson runs the ad agency. He's the bald guy near the band. See him? He's wearing a leopard skin."

Before Erica set off on her march toward Miles, a tall, slinky blonde approached them and plastered herself against Nick's body. "Nicky! Oh, I haven't seen you in so long. You look super. Let's dance."

"Nice to see you. But I really don't want to—"

"Yes, you do. You're a super dancer."

He looked toward Erica, and the blonde drew away. To Erica she said, "You don't mind?"

"Of course not. I don't think Nick wants to hear what I have to say to Miles Patterson, anyway."

"Well, aren't you the independent little thing!" She dragged Nick onto the dance floor. "Come on, Nicky."

Independent? Erica nodded. She was independent. She was going to Tanzania all by herself. And wasn't that swell! If she were a shy, clinging vine, Nick wouldn't be dancing with that woman. Nor would he look as if he were enjoying it.

Even as she watched, another female approached him, squealed and cut in on the blonde. Apparently, at one time or another, Nicky had made his mark among the sultry females of Denver. Probably in New York, too. He'd been a powerful stockbroker, a man of influence, an attractive man.

Mesmerized, Erica observed this mating ritual. Dancing. Cheek to cheek. Why did her independence suddenly feel like a cage? Though she wanted to storm the dance floor and assert her claim on Nick, she had no right to do so. He didn't belong to her. And now that she had received her grant, there was absolutely no possibility of a permanent relationship between them.

She stalked toward Miles Patterson. En route she encountered no less than three lovely models who were squirting samples of Safari perfume.

Erica firmly interrupted him. "Mr. Patterson. My name is Erica Swanson. I am a primatologist and a senior keeper at Golden Independent Zoo. I must protest the treatment of these animals."

He dismissed her with a wave of his hand. "Absolutely. I'll take it under consideration."

"Perhaps I should warn you, sir, that I intend to walk into the lobby and use the telephone to contact the ASPCA, the Humane Society, the Anti-Vivisectionist League, the Dumb Friends and the USDA. It might be bad publicity for your perfume to be cited for animal cruelty."

"What?"

"You are aware, aren't you, of the 1986 Animal Welfare Amendment, administered by the USDA?"

"I had no idea," he sputtered.

"You do now. These animals should be removed immediately."

"Yes, ma'am. I will take care of it." He spread his hands wide and glanced at his companions. "I had no idea."

"You have fifteen minutes," she said, checking her wristwatch. "Then I will place my phone calls."

Miles Patterson signaled to several people, and Erica placed a discreet distance between herself and the sputtering executive. Though she felt some satisfaction that this situation would be rectified, it was a small victory. Man's stupidity—more than intentional cruelty—was a constant amazement to her.

Her gaze wandered to the dance floor, where yet another female had attached herself to Nick. He was smiling, obviously enjoying the attention. Erica bit back her instinctive jealousy. She had no right. No claim. Nick was an eligible bachelor, and it was apparent that he fitted in well with this glittering crowd. She did not. Never had she felt so out of place. Never. She wanted to leave, to run home and bury her head under a pillow.

But she would wait until the animals had been taken care of. At least that long. Her wristwatch showed ten more minutes before she would make phone calls. Unfortunately most of her threats to Miles Patterson had been a bluff. Though there was an Animal Welfare Act that had been passed by both houses of congress in 1986, the regulations were not in place and enforcement was minimal.

Nick joined her. "Are you ready to leave?"

"I thought you needed to talk with your account executive."

"I just did. The redhead in the gold lamé sarong handles Barron's advertising."

"I see." Of course he would have a glamorous consultant. Beautiful women would always be falling over him. And she would be in Tanzania.

"I mentioned the animals to her, and she's going to talk to Miles."

"I already have," Erica said.

The animal cages were being moved, jostled through the crowd toward the rear exit doors.

A red-faced man in khakis stormed up to Erica. "Are you the one who talked to Patterson?"

She nodded.

"You've got a helluva nerve, lady. These are my animals, and they aren't being mistreated."

"Oh, no? And I suppose the cats weren't sedated for this party. And I suppose their claws haven't been clipped and their teeth filed." She could see from the flicker of guilt in his eyes that she was right. "And I suppose the loud music doesn't bother them. And the cramped cages. And the squirts of this wretched perfume in their faces."

"They belong to me. I can do what I want."

"I sincerely hope not. You're not fit to care for animals."

"You'd better not make more trouble for me."

"You bet I will. You can count on it."

He clenched his hands and moved aggressively toward Erica. Nick stepped between them. "The lady is right."

The red-faced man snarled. "Who are you?"

"Somebody who is going to put you out of business."

"I can handle this," Erica said to Nick.

"Let me," he said. "I have a solution."

"This is my fight." She was being unreasonable, but she was so keyed up she couldn't stop herself. "You have your own concerns, Nick. All these women who want your undivided attention."

"What?"

"Go back to your harem," she snapped. "I can take care of this scum."

"I'd like to see you try," the red-faced man growled. "If I want to take these animals out of here and shoot them, I can. It's my right. They belong to me."

"You won't do that." Nick's voice was cool and hard. "Because it's not going to do you any good."

"Nick—"

He turned to her. "I'll take care of this, Erica."

"Fine." She turned on her heel and stalked from the room.

The cages were gone. The animals had been given a momentary reprieve. That was all that she could do for them. Tomorrow she would contact as many animal protection agencies as possible, but she'd done all she could for tonight.

Out on the street she took a breath of clean, fresh air. And coughed. The cloying scent of Safari perfume clung to her. She wanted a bath—another long soak in a hot tub. She wanted to refresh herself, to wash away the tension.

But now she had to find her way home. Independently.

11

WHEN ERICA WALKED OUT of the party, it was nine o'clock on a Friday night, and the activity on the picturesque Sixteenth Street Mall had slowed to an easygoing pace. It was a lovely summer night, but the wafting breeze and gently glowing streetlamps did nothing to calm her. Mentally she raced through a litany of complaints—all directed toward Nick. Not only had he been inconsiderate by dancing with those other women, but she also despised his take-charge macho attitude with that disgusting animal handler. And she wasn't particularly pleased with his routine from yesterday, either. How dared he insist that her honor was at stake in fulfilling a nonsensical commitment, sealed with a pocketknife and a key.

With arms swinging vigorously, she charged past a couple who were strolling intimately arm in arm along the Mall. Erica looked away. She didn't want to see other people's happiness.

She marched past a sidewalk café where other couples talked and laughed, clinking glasses and smiling, enjoying themselves.

Why couldn't she be like them? Or like those women Nick had been dancing with? They at least had the good sense to be charmed and charming. Clever creatures, she thought. Those women exuded femininity without even trying. And Erica stood by in her pith helmet, raging war against an animal abuser.

Why was she so pigheaded? Her mother had been right. She would never find a mate, a true and loving mate, unless she learned to tone down her stubborn, willful nature.

But that would never happen. At least not with Nick. She left the Mall and found a bus stop. As she sat on the bench, her adrenaline rush began to dissipate. She took deep breaths and rotated her shoulders to ease her taut muscles, trying to tell herself everything had worked out for the best.

A horse and buggy clip-clopped along the street, and Erica was pleased to note that the horse was sleek and well tended. She was not so pleased to spy the couple in the carriage, staring tenderly into each other's eyes.

She slumped. Everyone in the world seemed to be in pairs. Everyone except her.

She and Nick were not in love, and she had to live with that fact. There would be no carriage rides or sidewalk cafés or moonlit strolls for them.

Peering down the street for the bus, she spied his Mercedes at the stoplight. Great. So he'd left his party early, and here she sat like a pathetic waif at the bus stop. She straightened her shoulders and attempted to look as if she always sat in the middle of downtown Denver after dark wearing a pith helmet.

His sedan pulled up to the curb, and Nick pushed open the passenger door. "I've been looking all over for you. Come on, Erica. Get in."

"You needn't worry about me. I'll take a bus. Feel free to return to your party."

"It isn't *my* party. If I'd known what was there, I never would have gone."

"You seemed to be enjoying yourself," she said archly. "And all those women were certainly enjoying *you*."

"Get in, Erica."

"No. I'm taking the bus."

He closed the car door and drove around the corner. At this time of night it was easy to find a parking place. He slipped in beside the curb, locked the doors and hurried back to the bus stop. She looked so small and lonely, he thought, sitting there in her khakis. "I thought you might want to know what happened with the animal handler," he said.

"Not at all. Like the dominant male you are, you said it would be taken care of. Who am I, a mere female, to mistrust your judgment?"

"I bought them. All the animals at the party and two ponies besides. I'm going to donate them to the zoo."

Her mouth fell open. "What?"

"Before you fly off the handle, hear me out. There's a decent cage for the gibbons, one where the chimps stayed before Primate Island was built. And behind the snakes there's an enclosure for the hyena. And of course ponies will fit in almost anywhere."

She nodded dumbly.

"The big cats might be a problem," he said. "But I intend to donate enough money to build an enclosure for them."

"You bought those animals?"

"You're not the only person with humanitarian instincts, Erica. I couldn't stand to see them mistreated. Probably paid too much. But I think it's deductible."

She leaped to her feet and hugged him. "You keep doing this. Just when I think you're an awful jerk and we're never going to get along, you turn out to be a good person. I'm so glad."

"So am I." He hugged her back. "Now, am I forgiven for dragging you to that dumb party?"

She disengaged herself, remembering the lesson she'd learned that night: He was not her man. They were not in love. She could not claim him. With a sigh she settled back on the bench. "It wasn't your fault."

"Good." He held out his hand to her. "Let's go and find someplace to eat."

Spending these limited moments with him offered a great potential for pain, and she didn't wish to be hurt. Though she wanted to go with him, to let herself go and forget the consequences, she practiced restraint. The lights of a metro bus were visible one block away and she stood. "I'm not really hungry," she said. "I might as well take the bus home and get a good night's sleep."

His hand dropped to his side. "Does this have something to do with the fact that I danced with other women?"

Absolutely, she thought. "Certainly not."

"You're jealous." His grin was as wide as a Cheshire cat's.

"Am not. After all, I have no claim on you. You can tango with whomever you please."

She took a handful of change from her pocket and climbed aboard the bus. Nick was right behind her.

At this hour of night there were only four other half-asleep passengers on the RTD bus to north Denver.

The bus started up, and Erica staggered down the aisle.

Nick staggered after her and plunked himself down on the seat beside her. "You are jealous, aren't you?"

She stared straight ahead.

"Admit it, Erica."

"All right, Nick. I have a twinge of envy in the presence of gorgeous, sophisticated ladies. What normal woman wouldn't?"

The bus stopped at a light.

"That's not what I meant," he teased. "You're jealous, because you're being possessive about me."

"Honestly, Nick. You're so vain."

"It's true, isn't it?"

He leaned back with a smug grin that irked her tremendously. The bus resumed its course. She vowed not to give him the satisfaction of knowing that he was right.

"I was wondering, Erica, is possessiveness a bonding characteristic in higher primates?"

She growled, aware that their conversation was arousing the attention of the woman seated two seats in front of them. And of the teenage boy sitting opposite her.

He continued. "You said that gibbons were monogamous. What about chimps? And human beings?"

"Stop it," she hissed.

"You know, it's too bad we didn't dance together." The bus stopped again, and it was very quiet when he said, "That music was your kind of loud."

"Wrong beat."

"Oh, yes, you're always marching to a different drummer, aren't you? It must make you mad that you feel jealousy like any other normal woman."

"All right," she snapped as the bus jolted to another stop. "I didn't like seeing you in the arms of other women, smiling at them, laughing with them. I didn't want to be independent. I wanted to march out on that dance floor and say, 'Beat it, he's mine.' But I can't. I can't say that. You don't belong to me, Nick. I'm leaving. I don't have the right to love you as much as I do."

Her hand flew to cover her mouth, and she stared at him with wide, frightened eyes. "I didn't mean that."

"You said it."

"But I didn't mean to."

"I'm glad you did."

She folded her hands primly on her lap. "Please disregard that comment. It was a mistake."

The bus started up again.

"Erica," he said loudly. "You said you loved me. And I'm glad you said it."

"Don't be silly, Nick. You're making a scene."

"I'm so damn happy." He moved into the aisle. As the bus jolted forward, Nick went down on one knee. Gallantly he clasped her fingers in one hand and placed his other hand over his heart. "Erica Swanson, I love you, too. With all my heart. I love you."

The other passengers on the bus burst into spontaneous applause. "Way to go, man," said the teenage boy.

"Thank you," Nick said. "I do love her."

Erica gazed into his gold-flecked eyes. Her cheeks were flushed. Tears welled up behind her eyelids, and she blinked them away. "You sweet idiot."

"I love you," he repeated.

The woman seated in front of them urged her, "Go on, dearie, tell him that you love him, too."

"I do," she said. "God help me, I love you, Nick Barron."

With a dramatic gesture Nick rose to his feet and yanked the stop cord on the bus. They descended the stairs amid congratulatory cheers from the people on the bus.

"Here we are," she said as the bus pulled away.

"Only a few blocks from where we started," he said. "Why do I feel like I'm on a different planet? In a different town?"

"Because it all looks new." She smiled up at him. "I love you, Nick."

Beneath the soft amber glow of a streetlamp he pulled her into his arms and kissed her. Their bodies fulfilled their words, yearning for each other with a sweet, endearing love.

"Shall I try to find a cab?" he asked.

"It's not far. Let's go over to the Mall and walk."

Holding hands, they strolled lazily down the Sixteenth Street Mall. Erica felt like waving to the people in the sidewalk café. She almost ran up and kissed the horse pulling its old-fashioned buggy. Lovers, she thought. She and Nick were in love—crazy, impractical, head-over-heels in love.

For once their conversation was in absolute accord.

"It's a beautiful night," he said. "The moon is waxing, growing more round and full every night."

"Do you keep track of the moon's cycles?"

"Sure do. The moon affects my garden at the amusement park. I know that sounds lunatic, but it does. There are moon cycles for harvesting and others for planting. After I've done all the proper scientific things, I rely on magical moonlight. And I'm also a great believer in the *Farmer's Almanac.*"

"My sisters used to tell me stories about the moon," she said. "When the moon is on the wane, it's time to get rid of things. That's the time to start a diet. When it waxes, wishes can come true."

"Did you wish to be in love?"

"Very much." She smiled up at him and squeezed his hand. "And to have my love returned."

"Such a wonderfully simple emotion. Why have we made this so complicated?"

"Because we're both too smart for our own good."

They strolled together in companionable silence while the waxing moon shed its benevolent light upon them.

But a seed of doubt had been implanted in Nick's brain. Now that they had admitted to being in love, what came next? Of course she would still be leaving for Africa in a few weeks. And she would be gone for a year.

Philosophically, he reckoned that a year was not such a very long time. Four seasons. Twelve months. Three hundred sixty-five days. A year would pass. Then they would be together for many more years. It wasn't that long.

Emotionally, a year sounded like forever. Especially during the quiet winter season when the park was closed and Michael was in school. This winter he had planned to start hydroponic gardening, maybe build another greenhouse at the back of Barron's. He would find things to do while she was gone. He was a big boy. He could keep himself amused.

He released her hand and slipped his arm around her slender waist, and she linked her arm around him. "That's kind of a reach for you, isn't it?"

She adjusted her arm. "There. I think we fit together very nicely."

"I can't argue with that."

Nor with anything, she thought. The two of them were being so agreeable it was almost laughable. But she didn't want to tease. She was in love, enveloped in a blissful, pinkish fog.

Maybe, she thought, she could cut short her trip to Tanzania. Certainly she could schedule visits to Denver. And she needed to keep up with her research project at the zoo. Two or three trips would probably be necessary. But very expensive. She could use the money in her savings account. That was a fair solution. The Adventurers' Club wouldn't have to foot the bill for her trips. She could pay for them herself. At least once or twice.

When they reached his car, they confronted each other. Simultaneously they spoke.

"I'll come back for visits," said Erica.

"I'll take vacations in Africa," Nick said.

They laughed.

"We'll work something out," he assured her.

"I guess we'll have to. After all, we're in love." She went up on tiptoe and kissed him lightly. "It was nice walking along the Mall, kind of romantic. I'm not a city-type person, and I don't think I've ever done that before."

"It was romantic, but I agree. You're definitely not a city gal."

A mischievous notion struck her. "Okay, Nick, let's you and me go find some real moonlight."

She directed him onto Highway 6 toward Golden, to the zoo. As soon as they stepped away from the zoo parking lot lights, she pointed heavenward. "Now that's real moonlight."

In the black velvet skies the moon seemed huge. Hundreds of stars twinkled above them. To the east they could see the amber glow of Denver's lights.

"This is another world," he said. "Your world?"

"I've been happy here."

She took his hand and led him up the hill toward the office building. When they neared the porch, there was a loud barking from inside the building, the lights went on and a scared voice said, "Who's out there?"

"It's okay, Tim," Erica called back. "It's only me."

A small, round man with a beard and a shock of blond hair that stood straight up was silhouetted against the office lights. He held a large German shepherd on a short leash. "You gave me a start, Erica. Who's that with you?"

"Just Nick."

"Hi, Nick." Tim's greeting was enthusiastic. "I surely am looking forward to Zoo Day. I'm going to dress up like a chipmunk."

"Those costumes can get pretty hot," Nick warned.

"Shoot, I don't care. How many times in my life will I get to be a chipmunk?"

Erica abstained from mentioning that Tim's everyday appearance wasn't too far from that of a furry rodent. "We're just going for a walk, Tim. You're doing a good job as watchman."

"Thanks. I'll take Dog back inside. Bye, now."

As they strolled past the office, Erica mumbled, "Heaven help us if there ever was a real intruder. Dog would wreak havoc with all the animals."

"But it's wise to have someone on the grounds at night," Nick said.

"Yes, I suppose it is. And convenient. Tim needed a job, and he's willing to work for what Amanda can afford to pay."

They hiked along the asphalt trail to the highest point in the zoo, the llama enclosure. There were no lights except for the stars and the waxing moon.

Erica led him off the path to an outcrop of rocks, where she sat down, hugging her knees and looking out over the zoo and the city of Denver beyond. The glittering display of light spread before them like diamonds scattered across the eastern plain. Nick sat down beside her, enfolding her in his arms.

"It's peaceful, isn't it? With all the animals resting."

A loud braying came from the farmlike area of the petting zoo. And an answering hoot-hoot resounded from Primate Island.

"Almost all the animals," he corrected. His gesture encompassed the land beyond. "And the lights of Denver."

"It's beautiful," she said. "From this distance it's hard to imagine that people live there."

"Like a reflection of the stars. You can't see the problems or the pain. Up here the wind in the pine trees muffles all other sound. You can't hear the laughter or the cries."

She snuggled against him. "You're concerned about that, aren't you? The cries of children. And the animals at that awful party."

"Especially the kids," he said. "I never used to think about it when I was in New York. But I'm around kids all the time at the amusement park. Maybe now I'm mature enough to realize how special they are."

"Do you want more children, Nick?"

"Yes." His response was swift and sure. This was a topic he'd obviously thought about. "First I want to do the right thing for Michael, to make him a real home. Then I definitely want children. Not necessarily my own offspring, but I would want to adopt. Or be a foster parent. Or something. Hey, it seems silly to be the amusement park Barron and not have a mob of kids to enjoy it."

He pushed her hair back from her forehead and gazed into her dark eyes. "What about you, Erica?"

"I haven't thought about it much. Maybe because I came from such a large family, I haven't been in a hurry to reproduce. Also, my career has kept me so busy that I never expected to have time for children. But, then, I never expected to fall in love, either."

"Would you want to have my child?"

She shifted her weight on the hard rock surface and looked out at the city lights. To carry his baby, to have his seed growing within her. Erica felt the earth beneath her and the stars above. A sense of being one with nature pervaded her senses, and her hand instinctively touched her flat belly. A child. A miracle. "Yes, Nick. I would."

He covered her lips with his and pulled her against him. His touched filled her with intense heat, but the soft breezes cooled her back with a purely sensual caress. As one they moved down from their rocky perch to a soft grassy clearing in the midst of pine trees. Nick pulled his dashiki over his head and spread it upon the grass for her. She knelt on his shirt, unable to take her eyes from him. The moonlight touched his hair and graced his shoulder, making wan shadows and highlights.

Still on her knees, she held out her arms to him, and he took a step toward her. Touching his trouser leg, she pulled him into an embrace, cradling her head against the warmth of his thighs. Her hands ascended his leg past his muscular flank to his waist, holding him to her.

Slowly he knelt. They faced each other in the dim light with cooling breezes whispering faintly around them. He held her face, gazing intently as if he intended to memorize her features. There was a new tenderness in his kiss— almost a reverence. "I do love you," he said.

"And I love you, Nick."

Quickly they undressed, and Nick arranged their clothing beneath her, forming a nest on the grass.

"These clothes are going to be awfully wrinkled," she said. "Like an unmade bed."

"Stop, Erica. Don't say anything practical." He settled her comfortably on the clothing. "Don't even move. I want to remember you like this. How beautiful you are in the moonlight."

She loved to hear him say things like that. His kind, loving words made her feel happy inside. Again she reached for him, and he nestled down beside her, his thigh protectively covering hers.

When he delicately massaged her breasts and tantalized the sensitive nipples, she marveled at the pure, natural sensation of inner warmth contrasted with the cool night air.

"Are you chilly?" he asked.

"Not when you touch me."

"Then I guess it's my duty to touch you more thoroughly."

Beneath a blanket of stars, they prepared to celebrate their love in the time-honored way.

His kisses were gentle yet arousing, and there seemed to be a newness in his caresses. Was this love?

She glided her hands over his bare shoulders. They belonged together, belonged to each other. They were in love, and she rejoiced in that wonderful possessiveness.

It was not at all confining. She drew him to her, reveling in the melting sensation as their bodies met and matched from shoulder to thigh.

When she spread her legs, welcoming him, she felt the dry earth beneath her toes. Soil, she thought, for planting and growing. To have his seed growing within her would be so good.

He entered her, and she clung to him, loving him, loving the magic he worked upon her. Slow strokes. Then faster. Their bodies glistened in the moonlight. Her small cries of pleasure mingled with the night's wind song. Their rhythm was familiar but new. Thrusting together, in perfect harmony, they soared together, until they became one with the stars.

After a long, heartfelt sigh Erica propped herself up on an elbow and gazed at him. She was so much in love. She needed no shelter from the night, only Nick's presence to warm her. His handsome physique was spread before her, and again a possessiveness surged through her. She didn't want any other woman ever to touch this body. Absently she stroked the hair on his chest.

"Are you grooming me?" he asked.

"Well, you have all this lovely fur. I can't seem to keep my fingers away from it."

"You've been hanging around the chimps too long, lady. You're beginning to pick up their habits."

"Not all of them. Actually I'm more gibbonlike in terms of a relationship. Monogamous. Although the chimps sometimes practice an interesting courtship ritual."

He groaned. "I suppose you're going to tell me about it."

"Absolutely." She tweaked a hair on his chest, then gently massaged again. "Sometimes when a female is in estrus, she and one male will go off together. Maybe for two or three months. When they return to the tribe, she's usually pregnant."

"Kind of like you and me," he said. "Except for the pregnancy part."

"Someday that could be arranged," she teased. "But I do hope the chimps are not altogether representative of our behavior."

"Why not? Going off together for a couple of months sounds kind of fun."

"Ah, but when this couple rejoins the others, there doesn't seem to be any massive display of affection between them. And as we've seen from Java and Lenny on Primate Island, the father doesn't particularly bond with his offspring unless the mother is absent. The family structure is very matriarchal."

"Fascinating," he drawled. "Should we try some more bonding and/or courtship behavior ourselves?"

"Nick, does our love change your mind about coming to Africa with me? Maybe just for the first few months?"

"Not a chance. I'll visit. But I would rather stay at home and keep the hearth fires burning."

She lay back in her nest on the soft grasses. Somehow it didn't seem right for them to declare their love, then separate for a year. She couldn't help thinking that she was making a huge mistake. One of the reasons her marriage hadn't worked was long separations while she and her ex-husband pursued their own interests and studies. In her experience being apart meant growing apart. Would their love survive? Even the brightest star dimmed with the passage of time.

She glanced over at him. He was so good-looking, and she'd seen the way other women crawled over him at that party. How could she ask him to remain faithful to her?

A cold fear pierced her heart. If she left him, he might not be here for her when she returned. And then what would become of her?

"I love you, Erica."

"Yes, darling. I love you, too."

If only those magic words would reassure all her doubts.

12

FOR TEN DAYS Erica had struggled to balance the preparations for her expedition with the demands of love. Now, with a combination of excitement and dread, she was beginning to see an end to both. Her departure for Tanzania would be in ten days, the last day of August. Wednesday of the following week.

She had only ten days to renew her passport, take the necessary immunization shots, gather first-aid supplies and pack her clothing and personal items. Not to mention cleaning out her apartment and arranging to store her furniture.

Plus she needed to work extra hard to integrate Sheena with the other chimps on Primate Island and to show Michael how to make journal entries. As if this overburdened agenda weren't enough, this was the week before the big Saturday promotional Zoo Day. And there was the additional problem of what to do with the animals Nick had rescued from the party and donated to the zoo.

And, of course, there was Nick himself. Erica juggled her schedule so that she could spend every possible moment with him. They ate dinner together, worked together and slept together. Though he maintained the routine of rising from her bed and returning to his home every night, their lovemaking was a superb expression of sensuality and sincere emotion. Erica was happy. Exhausted but happy.

On Thursday evening she and Amanda had finally coaxed the two leopards out of their tiny cages and into the vacant chimp enclosure, which had been refurbished and would be their temporary home. Erica leaned against the cool concrete wall of the new Cat House and slid bonelessly to the floor.

"Leopards," Amanda said as she collapsed beside Erica. "I started out with a couple of scraggly buffalo and a moth-eaten mountain lion. Now I'm the keeper of these marvelous cats."

Erica watched the two felines as they sniffed and explored. The former chimp enclosure had been divided with the same heavy wire mesh that formed the outer edge of their cages. That way each cat would have its separate space. The spotted leopard was so skinny that her ribs showed. The black was fat and lazy.

When the black cat made a ferocious leap toward the high windows at the rear of his cage, Erica was pleased to note that he fell short. "I think they're fairly healthy despite being mistreated. And both are young," she said. "Although there is no way I'm going to look into their mouths and check their teeth."

The black leopard stalked to the front of his new cage, glared at them with fierce yellow eyes and roared.

"You're handsome," Amanda told the cat. "Loud as you are, and even if you did just eat ten dollars' worth of raw meat."

"Have you decided on his name?"

"Not yet. The spotted lady is Baroness in honor of Nick, and thank goodness for his contributions. Otherwise I couldn't possibly afford these two."

"He claims that their new house will be completed in less than a month. How is that possible?"

"I've had the plans drawn up for years," Amanda admitted. "I've always wanted big cats. I love the way their muscles move beneath their skin, and the way they go limp with total relaxation."

"That is indeed an enviable trait. Wish I could relax. Lately I've been running like a lemming on its way to the sea."

"Not an apt comparison, Erica. You're not racing madly toward your doom but toward your future. Aren't you?"

"Yes, of course. But I have this problem, and his name is Nick Barron."

Erica took a deep breath and told Amanda everything, filling in the few blanks for the older woman. "And now I don't know what to do," she concluded. "I didn't want to love Nick, but it happened, and now I don't want to leave him for a day, much less for a year. But I can't bring myself to cancel the grant. I may never get another one, and this expedition to Tanzania is the opportunity of a lifetime."

"Don't look to me for an answer, young lady." She clambered to her feet and dusted off her backside. "Naturally I would be thrilled if you decided to stay here, but I understand about your career dreams. Still, Erica, I'm a romantic at heart, and I know that love is the most precious dream of them all."

Erica stood and gave Amanda a big hug. "If anybody else said that, I would accuse them of being grossly sentimental. But it suits you. And all the good that you do."

"There you go again, making me into Saint Amanda."

The black leopard roared again and batted his paw against the heavy wire mesh that separated them.

"That's my kind of attitude," Amanda said. She adjusted the heavy white bun at her nape and winked. "Surly but beautiful."

THE NEXT DAY, while Erica and Michael walked to the office to pick up Sheena for her afternoon session on the island, Michael spoke up. "Can we talk for a minute?"

"Sure, what's on your mind?"

"I've been thinking about your trip, and I'm really glad you're going." He shuffled his feet and stared down at them with apparent surprise, as if he had no idea how they were moving. "And I'm really, really happy I'm going to be in charge of the chimps while you're gone. But if something happened, you know, like if you somehow didn't go? Well, that would be real fine. You know?"

"Thank you, Michael. I think."

He punched her shoulder. "I'm going to miss you."

"There's a lot I'm going to miss, too." She gazed up at the cloudless sky and inhaled the arid Colorado breeze. She knew the vistas from the zoo like the back of her hand. It had been home to her for almost two years. The sights and smells were achingly familiar.

"I'll miss this place," she said. "And all the people. I'll have a lot to remember when I'm alone in the jungle."

"Yeah, well, I don't know if I should say this, but my dad is going to be a real pain when you're gone."

I sincerely hope so, she thought. *I hope he will miss me.*

ON SATURDAY Erica and Sheena were up earlier than usual. It was the Zoo Day promotion, and Erica was fatalistically sure of one thing: everything that *could* go wrong *would* go wrong.

They were halfway out the door, when her telephone rang. She retraced her steps and allowed Sheena to scamper around the apartment still attached to her leash.

"Hello?"

"I want you to come home, Erica."

"Mom? What are you talking about? Is something wrong?"

"No, it's just that you're leaving for Africa for a whole year, and I'd like to see you before you go."

Though Erica generally returned home for the holidays, she hadn't spent any extended time with her parents for years. With such a large family it was sometimes difficult to keep in touch, and her mother's sudden concern puzzled her.

"Erica?" Her father's voice boomed through the extension. "Erica, we're so proud of you, kiddo."

"Thanks, Dad."

"Listen, kiddo, your mother has been kind of gloomy. She keeps saying that she senses something wrong about your trip, like you're scared or you don't really want to go."

"I have second thoughts occasionally," Erica admitted. Occasionally? More like constantly. She couldn't stop worrying about what the trip would do to her relationship with Nick. "But I'm fine, Mom. Really."

"You don't sound fine. I'm sorry, Erica, but you sound unhappy. And I'm as agitated as a pregnant sow. You'll be all the way around the world, honey. And there are all those crazy uprisings, not to mention the diseases and the critters. Please stop off and visit for a day or two before you go."

That meant a day or two less time with Nick. But both her parents were in their late sixties, and they seldom asked her for anything. Erica bit her lower lip.

"Please, Erica, honey, don't be stubborn about this."

"Okay, Mom. I'll make the flight arrangements and let you know."

"Great," her father said. "I've got an invention out in the barn that you're probably going to want to take with you. Kiddo, it's a solar stove."

"How big?"

"I could squeeze it down to about four feet square. It's kind of like a kiln."

"Sorry, Dad, but I don't have space for toilet paper, much less a giant—"

"Is there a man in your life?" her mother interrupted. "Didn't you write to us about a young man who was working with you at the zoo?"

"Michael? He's sixteen, Mom." She paused. "But there is someone else. Michael's father."

"Oh-oh," her father said, "this sounds like girl talk."

"Dad, I'm not a girl. And neither is your wife."

"Love you, kiddo. I'm going out to the barn."

Erica heard him hang up the extension.

"His name is Nick . . ."

She told her mother everything. After she hung up, Erica was surprised at how much better she felt. Predictably, her mother leaned toward canceling the research and staying with the man she loved. Yet she acknowledged Erica's career needs. "It would be a shame to have come this far," her mother had said, "and not follow through."

A shame, Erica acknowledged. But necessary.

For the past week she had rolled the options around in her head and talked with people and made her itinerary and changed her plans so many times that the future was a murky mess of possibilities, but finally it seemed as though the sun had broken through. She knew what was the best thing to do.

She loved Nick. And she couldn't leave him. Monday morning she would call the Adventurers' Club and turn down their grant with profuse apologies. She would stay.

Sheena snuggled up in her arms, and Erica hugged the little beast. "And how could I leave you, Sheena? I promised myself you'd be buddies with Java, and I simply can't take off until that happens."

Sheena shook her head so vigorously her teeth rattled.

"Come on, Sheena. It's a big day today. Zoo Day."

It was the day she had chosen her love over her career. A very big event, indeed.

WHEN ERICA AND SHEENA entered Golden Independent Zoo, it was still an hour before opening time, but activity was fast and the atmosphere frenzied. Several of the volunteer zookeepers were already wearing their silly costumes. There was Tim the chipmunk. And two women in reindeer suits. Nick's organ-grinder outfit had been modified for a balloon seller who had inflated a dozen colored balloons with helium.

Nick had also recruited refreshment vendors from Barron's, offering snow cones, pretzels, popcorn, soda pop and hot dogs.

Amanda, wearing jodhpurs, high boots and a cowboy hat with a long yellow scarf tied around the brim, hurried toward her. "Thank God you're here, Erica. We have a crisis."

"It looks like everything is under control. A little nuts maybe, but under control."

"One of the snakes is missing."

"What?"

Amanda shushed her. "I don't want everyone racing around hysterically. Erica, you've got to find her. Patty the python is not in her cage."

"I'll take care of this," Erica said with a confidence she didn't feel. There were hundreds of places a python could hide.

"Please do," Amanda said briskly. "It would be dreadful publicity to have the zoo patrons eaten by an eight foot long snake. I'll take Sheena. You find Patty."

Erica handed over the leash and set out. Since Patty was shy, she'd probably slither away from the activity. The groundhog community, however, offered several tempting morsels.

As she neared the groundhogs, Erica bumped into Nick. He was dressed as a mime, with white gloves, a sleeveless black shirt, enticingly tight black trousers and whiteface.

"You like?" He struck a Marcel Marceau pose.

"Very appropriate to your love of quiet. But do you know anything about being a mime?"

He bobbed his head and gave a wide, gaping smile.

"Oh, really?" She laughed, wanting to hurl herself into his arms, to tell him she'd decided to stay with him. But now was not the time or the place. She had a python to catch, and he had a day's worth of entertainment to organize. "Later today," she whispered, "I have something special to tell you."

He pointed to his wide, dopey grin.

When she moved away from him, he tugged at her arm. "What is it, Nick? I really have to run."

He thumped his chest, drew a big heart in the air, then pointed to her.

"Let me guess. Does that mean 'I love you'?"

"You got it on the first try. And I love you, too."

She slipped her arms around him. "Mr. Mime, that goes without saying."

"Don't kiss me," he warned. "You'll ruin my makeup."

"By the way, did Amanda happen to mention our little crisis?" She innocently batted her eyelashes. "Patty the python is not in her cage."

"Oh, my God! Why are you standing here talking to me?"

"I was wondering the same thing myself."

He gave her a quick squeeze and released her. "Go. Hurry."

"Please don't tell anybody else, Nick. We don't want to start a panic."

"It's okay." He turned and headed for the safety of a crowd. "I'm panicked enough for everybody."

Her first step was to explore Reptile House, where she discovered that Patty's escape route must have been a loosened ventilation shaft. Patty was nowhere to be seen.

After grabbing a snake bag, Erica scouted the general area around the snake house, then widened her search. It wasn't until the gates opened and several zoo visitors entered that she spied the python, lurking in the high grass on the far side of the buffalo pen. Erica easily scooped up the big snake and slipped her into the snake bag.

"Crisis number one averted," she said to herself.

After she'd returned Patty to her cage and tightened the screws on the ventilation shaft, Erica found Amanda and informed her that prodigal Patty had returned. Then she went to keep an eye on the happenings near Primate Island.

Halfway down the hill, she was aware of being followed. When she swung around, she saw Nick, mimicking her every move. There were several children tagging along behind him, laughing at his hip-swinging imitation of Erica's gait.

She folded her arms beneath her breasts. "Cute," she said.

"Cute," he repeated, folding his arms.

"Mimes aren't supposed to talk."

"Mimes aren't supposed to talk," he parroted, and his audience of children giggled appreciatively.

Her eyes narrowed.

So did his.

She made a wavy motion through the air and hissed.

"Snake!" His face became an exaggerated mask of terror. He hopped on one foot, then the other. The children copied him.

He whispered to Erica, "There really isn't a snake, is there?"

"No, you clown. Patty is safely back in her cage."

The hug he gave her was friendly, but the grateful look in his eyes was definitely X-rated. "My heroine."

What would he do, she wondered, if she told him right now that she was staying in Denver? He would probably find a way to carry her off into the sunset . . . even though it was only 10:00. She turned to his audience. "I'm going to feed the chimps. Would you like to watch?"

"Yes!" they shouted.

Like fuzzy yellow ducklings, they fell into line behind her.

Nick brought up the rear. The Zoo Day was going well, he thought. The attendance was good so far, and he had noticed several people stopping at the booth Amanda had set up to sell zoo memberships and recruit volunteers. Though admission for today was free, he figured that the profit from the food concessions would be a very healthy sum.

Erica had reached the fence beside the moat and was lecturing. She was good with kids, he thought. Though she didn't play games or stand on her head, she had their attention. Maybe because she didn't talk down to them. When Erica discussed chimps, her inner enthusiasm shone through and captivated whoever was listening.

He drew a deep breath. She certainly had *his* attention. Damn. It would be harder than hell to let her go.

The rain forests of Africa? Damn. During the past week he'd been reading about the area and had discovered a fascinating abundance of tropical plant life that thrived in the unusual climate. Maybe when he visited her, he would take cuttings or seeds and attempt to introduce the rain forest vegetation to Primate Island.

Erica was now wading into the moat, dragging the food boat behind her. He watched the level of the stream creep above her knees to her thighs. There would be streams in Africa, he thought, but not safe like this one. There were crocodiles and a disgusting variety of snakes. If anything happened to her on this expedition, he would never forgive himself.

When she tossed the fruit and nuggets of food onto the island, the chimps appeared. Lenny, of course, got first pick. Then Jenny settled down to eat, selecting bits and flinging them to her son, Java. The baby ran off with a banana. She opened it carefully and ate the soft fleshy center, then began to chew on the peel.

Fortified by his morning feast, Lenny marched to the edge of the moat. He glared at the watchers, thumped his hairy chest and burst into a loud pant-hoot.

The kids loved his display, and Lenny launched into a real performance. Bouncing up and down. Making angry faces.

Java tentatively joined in, and Lenny actually encouraged him to make a hunched-shoulder swagger toward Jenny and the baby, a display that left Jenny unimpressed.

Erica had returned to shore. "I don't like the way they're behaving," she said to Nick. "They're too excited by all this attention. If you see Michael, tell him not to go onto the island today."

The children were laughing and yelling, and Erica turned around to see what was so exciting. A chipmunk in the moat. A very wet, human-size chipmunk named Tim.

The chimps reacted with absolute horror to the sight of this huge, furry creature. Jenny screamed and threw sticks.

Then Tim slipped. He foundered in the water until Erica fished him out and dragged him to the shore. "What do you think you were doing? Yuck, you smell awful."

"Sorry. It's just that this costume is so hot. I figured a dip in the stream might cool me off."

Nick appeared beside them. "Is everything okay?"

"Nothing wrong that a blow dryer can't fix." To herself, Erica muttered, "Crisis number two."

The third crisis happened after lunchtime when a teenage girl got her finger stuck in the wire mesh inside the new Cat House. Erica was near enough to hear the girl's shrieks and bolted inside. The volunteer keeper for the cats was doing an excellent job of keeping the skinny spotted leopard, Baroness, distracted with a piece of meat on the end of a stick, but he was unable to help the girl at the same time.

Erica stepped up to her. "Hold still," she commanded.

"Oh, God! It's going to eat my finger. Oh, my God!"

"Hold still and be quiet."

The girl whimpered but obeyed as Erica eased the overlapping wires apart. The wires were actually caught on the girl's ring, which fortunately had kept her finger from being injured.

"Okay," Erica said. "Very slowly pull your finger out."

The girl did. Once free, she pivoted and ran to the arms of her girlfriend, who had been watching with wide, terrified eyes. After the shock had subsided, Erica asked, "Are you all right?"

The girl looked at her finger and nodded.

"I'm not going to waste my time or yours lecturing about why you shouldn't tease the animals," Erica said firmly. "I'll have to ask you to leave the grounds."

"We can't."

"What do you mean, you can't leave?"

Her friend answered, "We didn't even plan to come to your stupid old zoo, but there was a guy at Barron's who was offering a free ride. We hopped on the bus with everybody else."

Erica groaned. No doubt Nick was responsible for hauling unwilling patrons from the amusement park, and that had to be one of the dumbest ideas he'd come up with. Surely there were enough people sincerely interested in attending a zoo without having to coerce them. "All right, ladies," she said to the girls, "if you get into any more trouble, you'll have to wait on the hot bus. Understood? Never tease the animals."

Three crises, Erica thought. With any luck three was a charm. The rest of the day would be fine.

Through the afternoon there were minor problems: someone trying to feed a snow cone to the buffalo, the camel spitting on one of the zoo patrons, and several lost children. It wasn't until near closing time that Erica encountered a personal crisis of such magnitude that the rest of the hectic day seemed as smooth as a pond on a windless day.

Near the llamas she spied Dr. Arthur Windom, the spokesman for the Adventurers' Club. Though she intended to turn down the grant on Monday, this was not a good time to present him with that particular problem.

She strolled up to the peppery little man. "Dr. Windom?"

"Right, hello," he barked. "It's you. Erica of the apes. Fine operation you have here."

"Thank you. Amanda does an excellent job."

"Indeed. She is an excellent woman."

They'd make a cute couple, Erica thought, despite Amanda's being four inches taller. "She's widowed, you know."

"Didn't know." He winked. "Thanks for the data."

"Dr. Windom, I'm glad I have this chance to tell you personally how much I appreciate the vote of confidence from the Adventurers' Club. It means a lot to me."

"Well, you're qualified. The project has merit. 'Course it didn't hurt that old Nick anted up, eh?"

"Excuse me?"

"Money for your grant. Seventy-five percent came from Barron. The rest of us couldn't be so mean as to refuse the last twenty-five, could we?"

Erica's heart sank to the soles of her feet. She hadn't achieved her career goal by herself. The grant was a present from Nick.

She forced her lips to smile, but she couldn't stand there chitchatting. Her instinct was to run and hide, to find a solitary place to lick her wounds. "Please excuse me."

"Right. And good luck in Tanzania."

Staring down at the asphalt path, she stumbled toward the office. What a fool she'd been! What a pompous fool! She'd accepted everyone's praise as her due, looked upon herself as a researcher to be reckoned with. But she hadn't won the grant at all. She'd received money as a gift from the man she was sleeping with. And what did that make her?

She closed the office door and sat behind her desk. The crowd of zoo patrons was beginning to thin. Soon they would be gone. It would be quiet, the kind of time that Nick enjoyed. Damn him! She took the pocket radio from her desk drawer, plugged in her headphones and turned the volume of the rock music station to high. She and Nick were opposites. He was happily settled, she was waiting for the adventure of her life to begin.

He must have realized that, too. He must want her to leave, to disappear into an African jungle. Thank goodness she hadn't told him she intended to stay. She would have really made a fool of herself if she'd told him she intended to toss away the grant that he had cleverly engineered behind her back.

She took her journal from the drawer and stared down at the blank page. Why couldn't Nick have left well enough alone? What did all these manipulations prove? Her own gullibility, for one thing. His need to dominate for another.

She felt a tap on her shoulder and swung around in her desk chair to confront him. He was still dressed as a mime. How appropriate! There was so much he hadn't told her. She turned off the radio and unplugged her headphones.

"All in all, not a bad day," he said.

"Speak for yourself."

"Anyway, I'll need to stop off at Barron's. Would you care to meet me there for dinner?"

"No, I need to help Amanda clean up around here."

"Okay, I'll be over at your apartment later."

She didn't want that, didn't trust herself to face him with his deception when they were close to her bed. "I'll meet you," she said. "At Barron's. Nine-thirty in your office."

When he leaned over her and kissed her forehead, Erica went rigid. She refused to give an inch because she knew he was willing to take more than a mile. He would steal her self-respect, her pride, her love.

"Is something wrong?" he asked.

Let him guess. "Nothing at all. See you later."

Beneath the mask of white mime makeup, she saw him scowl. Was he irritated? Good!

"By the way, have you seen Michael?"

She shook her head. "He was keeping track of Sheena today. Since her enclosure has become the Cat House, there isn't anyplace for her to play except the rear of the office."

"But he's not here?"

"Obviously not."

He went to the door, grasped the handle and turned back to her. "Are you sure nothing is wrong?"

"Nothing I can't survive."

From the start, she'd vowed to control the development of their relationship. But she'd been lulled by whooshing rides on the Ferris wheel, his laughter, his promises. And his lovemaking. Damn. At what point, what idiotic point, had she handed over the rudder and lost control?

One thing was for certain, she thought as she slammed shut her journal. It was now time to abandon ship.

13

A ROUND GREEN LEAF WAFTED down from an aspen and fell to the water. It floated, swirled in an eddy, then was whisked downstream. Nick watched its progress. A tiny boat, he thought, caught in powerful currents, unable to control its course. Sometimes he felt like that, but not often. Lack of control was not a sensation he found comfortable, but it was something he was feeling right now. Erica's mood baffled him. Earlier in the day she'd been bubbly. What had happened?

Nick stood across the moat from Primate Island. The zoo was now closed. The vendors were packing up their equipment, and the visitors had gone home.

His face was washed clean of the mime makeup and he was ready to be on his way, but he still needed to find Michael. Nick chose to wait opposite the island, knowing that his son generally went here at day's end for a final check on the chimps.

Erica hurried down the path toward him. Certainly he thought her behavior in the office had been odd. This was even more strange. He saw concern written on her face. And fear.

"What is it?" he demanded when she stopped at the rail beside him and peered across the moat.

"Michael," she said tersely. "I knew you were looking for him, so I asked around. Tim said he went over to the island."

"Is that a problem? He goes to the island every day."

"But today the chimps were nervous."

"What do you mean?"

"Dammit, Nick. I keep telling you and Michael and everyone else that chimps can be dangerous. Vicious, even. They bite. And Lenny is incredibly strong."

Nick stared toward the island. A horrifying mental picture flashed through his mind: Michael lying beaten on the island. Unconscious. Bleeding.

He swung his leg over the fence. "I'll go."

"Wait!" She caught his arm, and they both froze.

"What is it?"

"Look," she whispered. "Would you look at that?"

Sheena popped out from behind a shrub. She hunkered down on the shore opposite them and made her hee-hee-hee sound. Java appeared beside her. Tentatively he draped his hand over the top of her head.

Sheena bared her teeth, and Java snatched back his hand. Still, he was undaunted. He inched closer and began to groom her back.

She wriggled, then settled down. Her eyes took on a glazed look, and it seemed obvious that she was enjoying Java's attention.

From behind the same shrub Michael's head appeared. He grinned widely and very slowly raised his hand in a thumbs-up sign. Then he settled down again, making a very inconspicuous chaperon for Sheena.

Erica's eyes filled with tears. This was one of the most gratifying moments of her life. Finally, she thought. After all the months, the messes, the shrieking and the battles. Finally Sheena had joined the others. One tiny piece of the natural order had been restored.

Lenny rattled the trees behind them, and Erica held her breath as the big ape stomped along the shore toward the two younger chimps.

Sheena gave a hoot but didn't flee.

Lenny stood watching for a moment. He wrinkled his forehead, shrugged and shuffled back into the quiet of the island.

A tear fell from Erica's eyelashes. This was what she'd wanted, what she'd worked for. Yet a deep sadness overcame her. Sheena didn't need her anymore. Her little chimp companion had found a new home.

She wiped the tear from her cheek and swallowed hard as she watched Sheena and Java playing. "Goodbye, Sheena," she said softly. "I'm happy for you."

When Nick took her hand, she didn't protest. The emotional impact of Sheena's success overwhelmed all other thought. She allowed him to lead her to a wooden bench on the other side of the path, away from the moat. They sat, still able to watch the chimps but far enough away that they wouldn't distract them.

Erica felt a new onslaught of tears and dashed them away impatiently. "This is silly. I feel like a mother whose baby has gone off to kindergarten. I'm proud but sad. Because I know things will never be the same between us."

"Go ahead and cry, Erica. It's hard to lose a friend."

"Sheena is not my baby or my friend. She's a chimp."

"But there's a bond between you."

"Damn, I swore I'd never let this happen to me. I really tried hard to be objective, not to make Sheena into a friend."

"All you've wanted for Sheena is that she be happy."

"And she'll be happiest with her own kind."

He enclosed her in his arms, and she snuggled against his chest, ignoring his betrayal and his manipulations of her future. For the moment her desire for creature comfort exceeded her disappointment and rage. She needed to be held, to feel the closeness of another human being. "But she wasn't a pet. I never want to think about her as a pet."

"What was she? An experiment? Erica, I know you're a scientist, but you're also a loving woman, a person who cares. There's nothing wrong with that."

"Oh, sure, if I don't mind being hurt."

She sat quietly for a moment, wishing she hadn't spoken to Dr. Windom, wishing she were still cushioned from the hard truth with blissful ignorance. But she wasn't. She knew that Nick had lied to her, and she presumed that he wanted her gone to Africa. The only question now was whether she should swallow her pride and take the grant. Or refuse it. Either way, their temporary relationship was finally over.

She wasn't ready to face that bleak future. Not yet.

"There's something else, isn't there?" He tilted her face toward his. "Something you're upset about?"

She cleared her throat. Not now. She didn't trust herself to talk to him now.

"I know," he said. "It's the buses."

"The buses?"

"Yeah, I had the brilliant scheme that if we didn't have a good-size crowd, I could import people from Barron's."

"Right." She remembered the girl who had stuck her finger into the leopard's cage. "That was a ridiculous idea."

"Mea culpa. I admit it. There were plenty of people here without my interference. It was actually only one busload, then I told the driver not to worry about any more."

It occurred to Erica that this situation was not incongruous with the way he'd arranged her grant. "Why, Nick? Why do you have to manipulate everything?"

"My intentions were good. I wanted Zoo Day to be a success."

"But if you'd asked Amanda or me, we would have said no."

"That's why I didn't ask. I'm used to taking charge, making decisions. When I see something that needs to be done, I do it and worry about the consequences later."

"How can you do that? It shows such disregard for other people's feelings. Nick, you have to trust people to come up with their own decisions. To live their own lives."

"Aren't you overreacting? I said I was sorry."

"I know." She felt the impetus go out of their conversation. If she was to confront him about the grant, it would have to be clear and direct. It wasn't fair to hide behind another issue.

"But you're right about trusting people to make their own decisions. Michael is teaching me about that."

"What about Michael?" She was immediately defensive, too defensive. "He's done a wonderful job with Sheena."

"I think he's found his calling." Nick gazed over at the island. "I'm a little disappointed, I guess. Somewhere in the back of my mind I'd always hoped he would want to work with me at Barron's."

"That's a bit patriarchal, isn't it?"

"Very definitely," he admitted without shame. "But I always wanted to take him up on the roller coaster, gesture grandly and say, 'Someday, my boy, all this will be yours.' It takes away from the drama if he says to me, 'Dad, do I have to?'"

Despite her pain and confusion, Erica laughed. Lord, he was good for her. Amanda had been right when she said that Erica needed somebody fun loving to balance her overly intense approach to life. If only things had worked out between them.

"Michael's growing up fast," he said. "He's going to have his own life. And I'm going to miss him."

"A good father knows when it's time to let go."

"I know. But it's tough. Maybe because I haven't always been a good father."

She stared at him in disbelief. No matter what else he was, Nick Barron easily qualified as Father of the Year. "Come on, Nick. I've seen you in action with the handicapped kids and with lots of others. You're wonderful with children."

"That came with age," he said. "But you wouldn't believe what a callous son of a gun I used to be. Back in New York when I was making big bucks on Wall Street, I couldn't have cared less about kids. And that was too bad because I missed out on a lot when Michael was a little boy."

She didn't believe the cold portrait he was painting. Certainly people changed with age, but they didn't completely reinvent themselves.

"I've been meaning to tell you about this," he said. "It kind of explains why home and family are so important to me."

She settled back to listen, hoping to find a reason to forgive him.

"We had a house in Connecticut, but I seldom went home, except for weekends, because there was always some big deal, some vitally important business—"

"Some excuse?" she interrupted.

"Yes, some excuse that kept me away. So I'd show up on a Friday night, maybe throw the football around with Michael on Saturday. By Sunday I'd be thinking about Monday. And money. I thought if I made enough money, the fathering part would take care of itself. Then Michael's mother and I divorced."

"I was so blind," he continued. "I didn't understand what had gone wrong. Keep in mind that I was at best a part-time husband and father. I was too absorbed in myself and my career to notice I wasn't paying attention to my family."

"I know the feeling," she said softly, thinking of her own career choices.

"Anyway, after the divorce I discovered how much I missed being Michael's father. I tried to spend as much time with him as possible and even took an apartment in Connecticut. And his mother was very flexible about the joint custody... until she received an excellent job offer in California. I could have fought the custody agreement, but she was determined and I didn't want to put Michael through a court battle. My boy was moved a continent away from me."

He paused for a moment, and Erica wondered if he saw the parallels. Separations, she knew, were difficult. And he should know that, too. Excuses led to neglect. This was blatantly obvious to her. Was it possible that he didn't see it?

"And then?" she prompted.

"I went a little crazy. That was about four years ago, and I began a personal quest to date every beautiful woman on the Island of Manhattan. There were parties every night. And ladies. Models and actresses and executives. They were gorgeous, and not one of them was a companion for

me. How could they be? I wanted somebody to make up
for the loss of my son. I wanted a family."

He gave a short, bitter laugh. "I was so desperate for a
family that I finally came home to Denver—after my father died—to take his rightful place at Barron's, the family business."

"That was two years ago. Michael was fourteen."

"Then came the most terrifying experience of my life.
Michael ran away from his mother's home in California."

"Oh, Nick. That must have been terrible."

"For two days he was out of contact. The worst part was
not knowing, being so helpless. I hired private detectives
in three states to search for him. And I sat by the telephone, praying that my son would call, knowing that I
might lose him forever. During that hellish wait I made a
lot of decisions.

"I knew that career wasn't the answer for me. Or a wild
social life. Or money. Or power. It was family, and Michael was my family. From the pain, the possibility of los-
ing him, I learned what love really meant."

He turned Erica's face toward him and gazed into her
dark brown eyes. "I never dreamed I would have another
chance, never dared hope I could find a real family. Father and mother and children. When my divorce was final, I thought I'd blown it forever."

When she looked away from him, he knew something
was wrong. He'd sensed it before, but now he was sure.
And it wasn't that incident with the buses from Barron's.

In her posture he recognized anger and fear. But why?
For one painful second he saw his relationship with her
slipping away. "Erica?"

"What happened with Michael? How did you find
him?"

"He telephoned from Phoenix. He'd taken a bus, and Phoenix was as far as he could afford. He stopped there and tried to work up the nerve to hitchhike the rest of the way. Thank God his common sense won out and he called instead."

"But why did he do it?"

"This trip of his wasn't just a lark. He wanted to live with me for a while. He left without telling his mother because he didn't want to hurt her. But he wanted to be with me."

Nick glanced back at the island. "He'll soon be ready to leave me, too. Ready to set out on his own life. And I thank you, Erica, for giving him a direction. Even though it hurts like hell, I know Michael has to find his own path."

She covered his hand with hers and patted it. "He has a very good father to help him."

They saw movement on Primate Island as Michael slowly edged his way toward the stream and headed back across. He'd managed to slip away without attracting Sheena's attention.

As Michael crept onto the shore and started toward them, Nick whispered to her, "Tonight at Barron's. Half-past nine. There's more that we need to talk about."

"Yes, Nick. A lot more."

Michael stood before them like a conquering hero. "It worked," he said.

Erica embraced him. "Good job."

"You know what happened? Sheena was real crazy with all the Zoo Day stuff going on. And I tried staying with her in the office, but she hated that. Then I took her for a walk up on the hill. But she was still real weird. So I figured, 'Hey, maybe she's desperate enough to hang out with Java.' And she was."

"For future reference, it's not a good idea to go near the chimps when they're so excited," Erica told him. "But I won't put a damper on your success. What do you want to do next with Sheena?"

He beamed. "You're asking me?"

"Absolutely. You're the guy who got her to stay on the island."

"Well, I thought I'd get a sleeping bag and bed down on the shore on this side. So I could keep an eye on what's happening. And I'd be there if Sheena needed me."

Erica nodded. "Exactly what I would suggest. But, Michael, if there is a fight among the chimps, you are *not* to venture into the middle of it."

"What do I do?"

"Get yourself a ton of bananas. Food will usually distract them. I mean it, Michael, don't tangle with Lenny. He could really hurt you."

Nick stepped forward. "You understand that, son?"

"Yes, sir, I do."

Nick held out his hand, and Michael clasped it. The two Barron men stared into each other's golden eyes, then Nick pulled his son into a clumsy bear hug.

Erica could see that Nick was fighting back tears, and she finally understood his intense commitment to family. This father-son bond had been forged by separation and pain. These few years before Michael left the nest were Nick's last chance to be a father. Or were they? She was puzzled. How would Nick's family devotion affect her?

The hug ended with both men patting each other self-consciously on the back.

"Congratulations, Michael. I'm proud of you."

"Thanks, Dad. You know, I'm proud of me, too."

"Okay," Nick said. "I'm out of here. Erica, I'll see you later. Michael, be careful tonight."

Erica watched him stride up the hill, then quickly looked away. "Michael, go find a sleeping bag and bananas and food for yourself. Then come back here, and we'll go over some of the things you might want to watch for."

He dashed up the hill, catching up with his father and passing him. Nick turned back toward Erica. "He's on his way," he called to her. "Moving fast."

"Should we tell him to slow down?"

"It wouldn't do any good." He waved and continued along the path.

He was right, she thought. Everybody was entitled to make his or her own mistakes. But maybe—with experience and thought and a cool head—maybe she could avoid making another.

While she waited beside Primate Island for Michael to return, she pondered her future, examining every angle of it, every facet.

If she were being logical, she would accept Nick's charity and go to Africa. Following that scenario, she doubted that their relationship would withstand the separation. But her career would be beautifully launched.

Her innate stubbornness urged her to throw the grant back in his face. By working hard and applying herself, another grant would come along. And she would have the satisfaction of knowing that she'd earned her opportunity.

Another possibility became clear, and it gleamed enticingly. She could forget that she'd spoken to Windom and proceed with her early-morning decision to stay with Nick. To become the family he yearned for. But then her own dreams would be gone.

She gazed across the moat at Primate Island. Why was this decision so complex? On the opposite shore she saw Sheena and Java sitting side by side and staring at each other with bright black eyes.

14

AT TWENTY MINUTES PAST NINE Nick closed the accounting books. Deposits had been made, receipts filed, and everything balanced. Everything always balanced. Though it had taken a year to untangle the haphazard business procedures of his father, Barron's was now running like clockwork. Nick could leave for a month, and it wouldn't make the slightest bit of difference.

More than a month, he thought. He could find a way to leave for six months, a year. It wasn't the business of running an amusement park that kept him from going to Tanzania with Erica.

Why, then? He loved her. She was the missing piece in his picture of idyllic family life, the only woman in all the world he wanted for his mate. Why shouldn't he go with her? Because he wanted her here. This was his home, the place he'd fought coming to, the place where he now belonged. Home. His anchor. His stability.

Besides, Michael had a year of schooling left. Nick couldn't up and leave while his son was still in high school. He'd missed so much of Michael's upbringing and never wanted to be an absentee father again.

Nick left his office and stepped into the cool night air. He shivered, but the weather had nothing to do with his chill. Erica was leaving. Today was Saturday, and she was leaving on Wednesday of the following week. He shivered. His world would be an icy, barren place without her.

He strolled down the tulip-lined path away from his windmill office. Barron's closed at nine o'clock, and he could hear the last patrons being whisked through the exit gates. His employees would be gone soon after. There were two night watchmen who patrolled the grounds after dark, but otherwise he would be alone in the park. He and Erica would be alone here.

Why had she wanted to meet him here? Why not her apartment? Earlier today she'd mentioned a surprise. Nick sat on a bench beside a catalpa tree and waited. Barron's remained well lit at night, though the neon and the sparkling lights on the rides were dimmed. And the music no longer played. It was so still he could hear crickets chirruping.

Erica, who had changed from her zoo uniform into a red cotton blouse and slacks, came through the gates to Kiddy Land, and he smiled when he saw the swift determination evident in her stride. Obviously, he thought, this female didn't know the meaning of "quit." And that was one of the traits he loved in her. Her dedication. Her fearlessness. And the huge amount of love she carried inside, enough concern and caring for the whole world.

"Erica," he called. "Lady in red."

She started, then peered through the trees. "Why are you lurking under the catalpa?"

"This isn't a lurk. It's a wait." He patted the bench beside him. "Come on over here and sit."

She remained standing, hesitant. "I've never been here after closing. It seems bigger. I like it."

"How's Michael doing with Sheena?"

"Wonderfully." Her voice vibrated with enthusiasm. "I left about an hour ago, and it looked like the chimps were going to make their sleeping nests and nod off without any problems. I made sure that Michael was cozy in his sleeping bag, but I doubt he'll sleep a wink. He's so excited."

"And so are you."

"I am. I'd almost given up hope. I'm so glad Sheena has found her home."

"I'll bet Java is awfully pleased, too."

"Really, Nick. Those little apes are much too young to be thinking what you're thinking."

He got to his feet and approached her, placing his hands on either side of her slender waist. "What am I thinking?"

"I don't even have to guess." Her dark brown eyes met his, then glanced beyond his shoulder, avoiding him. "Is it okay if we take a tour of Barron's? I'm fascinated by the way it looks at night."

He backed up a step and studied her expression. Anger? No, he decided, she wasn't angry. Fear? Maybe. There was something about the set of her mouth that looked unhappy. "What's wrong? When you said you had a surprise for me, I assumed it was something pleasant."

"It was. At least I thought it was. But it isn't anymore."

"Is this a riddle?"

"No, I won't play games. I never wanted to say one thing and mean another, to trick you or deceive myself." She clenched her fists and drew them close to her breast as if holding something back, something important. With an effort she uncurled her fingers and allowed her arms to fall to her sides. "Walk with me for a while, and I'll find the words."

He fell into step beside her. His long-legged strides easily matched her more vigorous gait as they followed the winding path through flowers and forests at Nick's park.

Erica came to a halt when she beheld the carousel. In the pale moonlight the enameled stallions with flowing manes and flying hooves were magnificently unreal. These fantastic creatures towed ornate carriages, and their golden posts shone dully. Large mirrors in the curlicue design of the roof reflected the glow from distant stars.

"How lovely," she said. "They seem to have a life of their own after dark. Like the fantasy that toys and dolls stand and dance when the lights are out and the door to the nursery is closed."

"Is this your surprise? That Erica the realist has fantasies?"

"It is unusual for me." She neared the carousel and reached up to stroke the flared nostrils of a blue-and-yellow pony. "Obviously I've been spending too much time with you, and your attitudes have rubbed off."

"Too much time?"

She stepped onto the carousel platform and turned to face him. "I know about the grant."

"Well, I certainly hope so. You're intending to leave next Wednesday."

"I spoke to Dr. Windom, and he told me you financed seventy-five percent of the grant money. Is that true?"

"Yes."

With his single word her pulse seemed to still, her breathing to stop, her vital signs to cease. Then they resumed with a hard-driving fury. Her heartbeat thudded so loudly she was momentarily deafened. He had admitted it. Her last hope, that Windom had been wrong, was gone.

"Why? Why didn't you tell me? I've been marching around like a conquering heroine, patting myself on the back for being such a brilliant researcher. And it's not true. You've made me a liar."

"If I'd offered the money to you directly, would you have accepted?"

"Please don't answer my question with another question."

"Would you have?"

"Probably not."

"There's your answer. I wanted to help you achieve your dream, to give you the thing you most desired. And the Adventurers' Club seemed a logical means to that end."

"But you tricked me." She was aghast. He was treating this act as if it were nothing, a trivial matter. "You purposely deceived me."

"What difference does it make? You're getting what you've always wanted. You want an expedition to Tanzania, don't you?"

Her fingers tightened on the worn leather rein of the carousel pony. Her voice made the barest ripple in the still night. "I'm not sure that I do."

"What?" He stepped onto the carousel beside her. "That's all you've been talking about since we met. A field trip to Africa. Chimps in the wild. Primatology. Ethology."

"This morning I'd made a different decision." She moved away from him on the circular platform so that the flank of the enamel pony was between them. She wanted to mount the painted stallion and ride far away. "That was my surprise, Nick. I was going to turn down the grant so I could stay here with you."

"Oh, my God." He reached across the saddle and caught her hand. His grip was hard and tight. "Erica, don't tease about this."

"I'm not."

"How could I accept that decision? You once told me that a great difference between us was that I was semi-retired and you were still waiting for your life to begin. How could I ask you to wait? To give up your dreams?"

"You couldn't ask for it. Or demand. Or manipulate. My life belongs to me, Nick, and my course must be freely decided. Like a gift, it's something I would have given because it would bring me pleasure, too."

"And you would do that for me?"

"Not anymore."

She whirled around and walked away from him, picking her way through the fantastic carousel beasts. "I wanted honesty from you. 'Trust me,' you said, and I've trusted you. And you've made me a liar, a phony, a sham. Amanda is proud of me. My parents are so proud. What would they think if I told them my grant didn't come as a recognition of my work in the field but as a result of my efforts in the bedroom?"

"You can't believe that."

"What else can I believe?" Her footfalls clattered on the metal platform as she circled the carousel, touching the manes of the moonlit horses, grasping the golden posts. She moved round and round endlessly as if in a dream— a nightmare. But she knew she wasn't sleeping. She would not awaken from this moment. "Why else would you go to this very great expense, except as a kind reward for my favors?"

"Because I love you."

"And your way of showing this love is to ship me off to the other side of the world. Did you simply wish to be rid of me? Is that it, Nick? Are you so terribly bored?"

"You're being ridiculous, Erica. Of course I don't want to be away from you, not for one minute. This separation is going to be hell for me. Dammit, Erica. Will you stand still?"

She halted. "If you don't want to be separated, prove it. Come with me."

"Is that a dare?"

"I'm not playing games, Nick. You manipulated me, getting me that grant and letting me think I'd earned it. I will not be manipulated again. Or tricked. I want a simple answer. Will you come with me to Africa?"

"You know I can't."

"Why not?"

He was approaching her through the ornate painted creatures. Instinctively she kept a distance between them. If he caught her, she would be impaled as surely as these carousel ponies, frozen in a position of flight and unable to move. If he held her, she would lose control of her own destiny. "Why not? Why can't you come with me?"

"I have responsibilities."

"Barron's would run by itself. You're the one who told me that. Besides, the park is closed six months during the winter."

"There's Michael's schooling to be considered."

"Michael is deeply interested in a career in ethology studying animals. Surely an expedition like this would be of tremendous value to him. A field study. The details could be worked out with his high school."

"Maybe so, but I want to make a home for him, a place where he feels secure."

"Home isn't a place, Nick. It's the people who love you."

As she gazed at him, her strong resolutions faded. He was the only man she'd ever wanted so desperately. Yet they were destined for divergent journeys through life. "We've known from the start that we were very different."

"But we fell in love, anyway."

"Deluding ourselves."

"No, Erica." He caught her hand and dragged her toward him. "This is no delusion."

Roughly his arms closed around her, forcing her body against his. "You can't deny this, Erica."

"Stop it, Nick."

"It won't stop. Can't you feel it? Feel how right our bodies are together. It's not a lie, it's not a trick, and it sure as hell isn't a delusion."

A terrifying sense of absorption overcame her. Her separate will no longer existed. She was impelled toward him, drawn by his strength, and she loved this strength, adored and feared it. When her mouth met his, there was no logic. Only the intense flare of her emotional, physical response. Her lips moved against his, tasting him, yearning for him.

She wanted to give up this fight, this stupid fight. It would be so much easier to surrender to his will, to become an intrinsic part of him. Did that mean she had to lose herself? She'd always made her own decisions, and she was tired, longing for the relief of final capitulation.

She clung to him with every sinew in her body, holding tightly, so tightly that the moment seemed suspended. Would this be their last embrace?

She forced herself away from him. "No," she cried. "We can't do this."

"Why not?" He stretched out his hand toward her. "Why can't we continue as we were?"

"Being separated, on opposite sides of the world? Is that what you want?"

"Of course not. I'd rather be with you, but I want you to have your chance, to fulfill your dream."

"And how can you presume to know my dreams?"

She took his hand and pulled him to the inside edge of the carousel platform. They descended to the center of the ring, where the operator controlled the ride, and Erica pointed to the mirror that reflected both of them. "What do you see?"

"You. And me."

She turned to face him. "And now what do you see?"

"You."

"I'm not part of you, Nick. Not an extension. The only way I can join with you is of my own free will. My decision. My dream. You can't make me do what you want. Don't you understand? It won't work. Because I am not you."

She braced herself against a lever, feeling the weight of her words, and the lever moved. A loud blast of calliope-type music sounded, and the carousel began to turn.

"What did I do? What happened?"

"It's okay, I can turn it off."

"No, leave it. It's perfect."

She sidestepped him and hopped onto the circling carousel. In the darkness the horses bobbed up and down eerily.

She mounted a silvery-white horse. "Don't you see, Nick? The ponies only move when somebody turns on the motor."

"What?" he shouted over the music. "I can't hear you."

The wind whipped through her hair, and the ride went on. Around and round on a merry-go-round, she thought. This was what she feared—she would become nothing more than a stiff painted pony, paralyzed until he flipped the switch. Her love for him would rob her of will. And her life would be as predictable as an endless carousel ride.

But Nick had never forced her to do anything she hadn't wanted to do. In fact, he respected her stubbornness so much that he'd resorted to devious manipulations. Was the result the same? A sudden perception hit her. Her mind was still as she bobbed up and down and went round and round. Nick had given her a chance at the brass ring—the expedition. And she must take it.

She dismounted the silvery horse.

He switched off the machinery, and the calliope music died with a discordant wheeze. The ponies gradually slowed.

"You were trying to do what I wanted. That's why you set up the grant."

"I still can't hear you," he called back. "This damn loud music is still ringing in my head."

"But it only makes sense if you want to come with me."

She stepped off the carousel. If he came with her, it meant they wanted the same thing: a life together. If not . . . well, she had her career, and he had his home.

"Nick," she shouted, "I'm going to Africa. I'm going to use the grant."

"Good." He hopped off the slowly circling platform and came toward her.

"But I want you to come with me. If you don't, there's no hope for us. I know there isn't. We'll grow apart, become bitter, blame the other for not being there. We have to both want this relationship." She gazed up at him, wanting to take him into her arms, into her life. "Please, Nick, say you'll come with me."

Behind him, the carousel stopped. "Try to understand, darling. I can't."

"What you mean to say is that you won't. You can come. It is possible. But you won't. You're choosing not to."

In the instant when their eyes met, she felt all the pain of their future separation. Panic clawed at her throat, and her voice seemed shrill. "Please, Nick. I'll compromise. I could break the grant into a two-year period. Spend six months there. Then six months here. Then back again."

"I'd like that."

"But you have to come with me." She saw refusal in his eyes and continued frantically, hiding from his final refusal. "You could do your own work, your own botanical project. You wanted to take cuttings, to see if you could transplant the rain forest. Oh, please come. We have to be together."

"Erica, try to understand."

"No. I won't hear it. I won't hear you say no."

She backed away from him and hurriedly retraced her steps along the winding path through looming trees and spidery ferns. Then she was running. No longer an enchanted moonlit place, she fled from her future.

She burst into an asphalt-covered clearing and ran toward Kiddy Land.

Nick was right behind her.

He snagged her arm and pulled her up short. "Erica, stop. You're going to stumble and hurt yourself."

In a quick reflex she yanked away from him. They stood facing each other, panting.

"Listen to me. I love you, Erica. I want you and me and Michael to become a family."

"So do I."

"But a family needs a home. A peaceful place to live."

"I don't want to hear this."

She pivoted away from him. Her headphones and a truly loud tape were what she needed, something to drown

out the inevitable words she didn't want to hear. She spied
the control box for Kiddy Land and went over to it.

"Now what are you doing?" he asked.

"I'm striking up the band." She'd seen him operate this
area before and knew it was easy. Flipping open the metal
cover of the box, she touched three buttons, and, like
magic, Kiddy Land crackled to life, bathed in neon lights.
Several nursery-rhyme tunes played harmoniously.

"Erica, would you settle down and listen to me?"

"No, I won't. I can't settle down, not now. I need noise."
She nonchalantly strolled to the child-size motorboats
bobbing in a tank. "'Rub-a-dub-dub. Three men in a tub.'"

She reached over to the switch and started the ride. Then
she started the mini Ferris wheel and the bright little cars
that circled under a yellow-and-red striped canopy. And
a little motorcycle track. And the kid-size airplanes. Only
then did she return to Nick.

"Why did you do that?" he said, speaking loudly over
the cacophony.

"I needed a sense of control."

"We can't talk seriously in the middle of a 'Little Bo Peep'
song."

"There's no need to talk. All you have to do is say, 'Yes,
Erica I will go with you.' Later we can work out the details. I don't *have* to leave on Monday."

"I thought your departure was Wednesday."

"I'm going to Wisconsin for a few days to visit my parents."

She glanced over her shoulder at the cheerily spinning
rides. The giddy noise and action were enough to divert
her from the pain and fear she felt inside.

"Monday," he said. "The day after tomorrow."

"Say you'll come with me. We can figure out a compromise."

"But you're not talking about a compromise," he said, more loudly than he had to. "You're saying that I should leave my peaceful, settled-down life and follow you into a damn jungle. Lady, you are asking me to give up my warm bed, good food and decent transportation. You're asking me to give up the Sunday newspaper and sleeping late and soda pop. What about you? Doesn't this compromise work both ways? What are you giving up?"

Everything. Nothing. She didn't know what to say. The whirling rides seemed to be going faster and faster. She blurted out, "We're both getting something. A life together."

"Think about it," he said. "You've made me into the villain, the evil guy who tried to manipulate you, but I'm not the one who's dead set on disappearing into a jungle."

She blinked hard, trying to still the twirling lights. The moment of decision had come, the moment of truth when her future—their future—would be set. Her knees felt weak, and she was dizzy. Her arms didn't have the strength to hold him, and he was slipping away, disappearing.

"I'm sorry, Erica. I won't go with you."

He turned and slowly walked away.

She was left alone in the middle of the amusement park with the happy Kiddy Land rides blaring their simple tunes and the neon lights flashing.

15

ALL NIGHT THAT SATURDAY NIGHT Erica slept by the telephone, hoping Nick would call and tell her he'd changed his mind. But the phone didn't ring until Sunday morning.

"Hello?"

"Erica, this is Amanda. I have wonderful news to report. I have finally decided on a name for that sassy black leopard. I will call him Arthur."

"Arthur?"

"After that lovely gentleman from the Adventurers' Club, Dr. Arthur Windom. We spoke last night, and he'll be working with me on several ventures."

"That's terrific," Erica said fondly. "I'm glad there might be a special someone in your life. How's Sheena?"

"That's really why I called. All is well on Primate Island. When Sheena woke up this morning, she was agitated. So Michael fetched her. After about an hour she took him by the hand and dragged him back to the island, where she's been ever since."

"That is good news."

"Then why do you sound so dreadful? What's wrong?"

Nothing that could be fixed. "I'm a little nervous about my departure. I'll be leaving late on Monday instead of Wednesday. I'm going to visit my parents for a few days."

"If I can help, let me know." There was a genuine warmth in Amanda's husky voice. "We'll miss you, dear."

"And I'll miss you, too." Sheena, Patty the python, Amanda, Tim and everybody else at the zoo. Even the shaggy old buffalo. She would miss them tremendously. "Goodbye, Amanda."

Erica had a sense of closure, a feeling that natural order had been restored. Sheena had found her home, been reunited with others of her species. Amanda, the incurable romantic, was embarking on a courtship with Dr. Windom. And she, Erica, was alone again, setting off on her career.

Briskly she got to her feet. Spilled milk, she thought, and there was no use crying over it. An unbidden memory popped into her head: Nick teasing her about her farm girl wisdom.

Don't think about it. Later this afternoon she would go to the zoo for her real goodbyes, but now it was time for packing. After a shower and a vigorous brushing of her hair, she went to her bedroom and sorted through the contents of her closet. Most of her things were inappropriate jungle wear and would have to be placed in storage.

She stroked the yellow sundress she'd worn to the amusement park when Nick had taken her up on the Ferris wheel. And there was the conservative dress she'd worn to the Adventurer's Club. And the red slacks and shirt from last night. So many memories. Callously she whisked them into a garment bag and zipped it.

It was well past noon when she carefully began packing the glass animals on her shelf. She lingered over each, recalling the years of her life. Without a doubt this year, her thirty-second year, was the most eventful. There should be a huge glass something to commemorate it— during these past few months she'd found love, lost it and was about to leave for Tanzania. Perhaps a giant glass bubble, she thought, which she could hit with a hammer and break into a million shards.

That was the way she felt. Her fragile chance at happiness had been shattered. And she would be forever alone.

No one could replace Nick. No one would ever have his smile, his laugh or his crazy sense of humor. She would miss their teasing. Their silly differences. She would never again be able to listen to loud rock music without remembering how much Nick loved stillness. Never be able to drink a glass of water without thinking of his aluminum cans of soda pop. The word "home" would always have painful connotations for her. She sighed deeply and stared into a vague middle distance. No one would ever make love to her like Nick.

Very gently Erica removed her necklace with the imitation pearl pocketknife. Her fingers closed tightly around the small object, wishing she could somehow call him to her, summon him. But it was not to be. She wrapped the knife in tissue paper and placed it in the box.

No matter how hard she tried, Erica couldn't convince herself this was all for the best.

She wrapped a small glass chimp in tissue paper, then her hand froze. There was a sound. Maybe it was Nick opening the door with his key.

Happily she raced to the door. It was still closed. No one was jiggling the handle. But she'd definitely heard something. Some kind of banging or rattling noise.

She stood and listened.

A blast of music came from outside her kitchen window. What on earth was that? Kids with an incredibly loud stereo?

She went to the window and stared down on a ten-piece brass band in red-and-gold uniforms. They stood beside the tall cottonwood and played loudly.

She fumbled with the lock and opened her window to stare.

A barbershop quartet stepped out from behind the tree. To the band's accompaniment, they sang, "'Abba dabba dabba said the monkey to the chimp . . .'"

Erica clapped her hands and laughed delightedly. Who were they? Where had they come from?

The music stopped, and there was a tinny, tinkling melody.

Nick, dressed as a mustachioed organ-grinder, stepped out from behind the tree.

Erica felt an unbelievable happiness well up inside her. He was here. He'd come to her.

"Erica," he shouted. "Is this loud enough for you?"

The band sounded two booming, discordant notes.

Windows flew open all over the apartment building.

Erica put her hands over her ears. "I liked you better as a mime. Why are you doing this?"

"To show you I can compromise. I'll come with you to Tanzania," he shouted. There was a drumroll, then he continued. "If you'll shorten the expedition to six months."

"You've got it!"

"Then we come back here for six months."

She hesitated for a moment. Would this schedule disturb her research? No, not really. She could plan around it. Would it cause problems with the grant? Of course not. The grant was mostly from Nick.

Before she could shout her agreement, the drummer in the band rushed forward. It was Michael. "Please, Erica.

Dad said I could come on the expedition, but I'd have to make up school in the summer."

"Agreed," she shouted, "to both you and your father."

Michael gave a whoop of excitement and signaled the band. They began playing "Happy Days are Here Again."

Nick peeled off his organ-grinder mustache, discarded his music box and began climbing the cottonwood tree.

"Be careful, Nick." The man was crazy, wonderfully crazy, and she loved him.

Outside her window ledge he paused. "One more thing. Marry me tomorrow."

"Only if you're ready for serious bonding tonight."

He dove for the window and climbed inside. Leaning out, he waved to the band. They marched off, playing a joyful rendition of "Born Free."

He reached for her, resting his hand on her cheek. "I love you very much, Erica."

She kissed the palm of his hand. "And I love you, too."

They melted together, and Erica's world fell into place. This was the true natural order of things. They belonged together. "Married," she said.

"No second thoughts allowed."

"I wouldn't dream of it. You and me, buddy, we belong together forever and ever." She winked at him. "You may now kiss the soon-to-be bride."

He did, and she felt the rush of excitement all the way down to her toes. Through the baggy organ-grinder's costume, his firm body met hers in a passionate, committed embrace.

She leaned away from him, gazing up with dreamy eyes. "What changed your mind?"

"You. Something you said."

"Tell me, so I can remember to use if again."

"After I left you there in the middle of all those silly rides, I hurt. No place special, but all over. An aching. And it was sort of like when I was separated from Michael, but different. I realized that as much as I wanted a home, I couldn't stand to be apart from you."

"I'm glad." She went up on tiptoe and kissed him lightly. "But what did I say?"

"The truth, Erica. The honest truth. You told me that home wasn't a place. Home is being with the people you love."

A sense of fulfillment overcame her as she snuggled in his arms. Erica Swanson had found her mate.

Harlequin Temptation

COMING NEXT MONTH

Harlequin Temptation dares to be different!

Once in a while, we Temptation editors spot a romance that's truly innovative. To make sure *you* don't miss any one of these outstanding selections, we'll mark them for you.

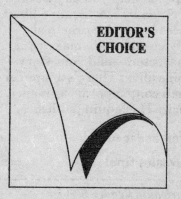

EDITOR'S CHOICE

When the "Editors' Choice" fold-back appears on a Temptation cover, you'll know we've found that extra-special page-turner!

THE *Temptation* EDITORS

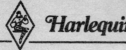

Harlequin Superromance

CALLOWAY CORNERS

Created by four outstanding Superromance authors, bonded by lifelong friendship and a love of their home state: Sandra Canfield, Tracy Hughes, Katherine Burton and Penny Richards.

CALLOWAY CORNERS

Home of four sisters as different as the seasons, as elusive as the elements; an undiscovered part of Louisiana where time stands still and passion lasts forever.

CALLOWAY CORNERS

Birthplace of the unforgettable Calloway women: *Mariah*, free as the wind, and untamed until she meets the preacher who claims her, body and soul; *Jo*, the fiery, feisty defender of lost causes who loses her heart to a rock and roll man; *Tess*, gentle as a placid lake but tormented by her longing for the town's bad boy and *Eden*, the earth mother who's been so busy giving love she doesn't know how much she needs it until she's awakened by a drifter's kiss . . .

CALLOWAY CORNERS

Coming from Superromance, in 1989:
Mariah, by Sandra Canfield, a January release
Jo, by Tracy Hughes, a February release
Tess, by Katherine Burton, a March release
Eden, by Penny Richards, an April release